RAYLA 2212

Ytasha L. Womack

D1713762

YSolstar

Chicago, Illinois

www.rayla2212.com

Contents

1

2212: Book of Rayla

p. 1

2

Rayla Redfeather

&

The Return of Bettye X

p. 61

3

Rayla's Revolution

p. 129

2212: Book of Rayla

1

Chapter 1

Once Upon a Time

The Book of Rayla ...

aka when Michael Jackson became a star in the sky Once Upon a Time

THE white light is a dagger in my heart. I press my breasts to the wet soil and pray that no one can see me. My sweaty palms are clasped over my tiny ears waiting for the piercing crackle of thunder, but it never comes. Where is it? A gust of chilly wind blows over me. I squint. In that flash, she appears. A sea of swaying yellow grass so high and so thick, it could only be the Field of the Yellow Lady. Like a thirsty woman in a desert, who craves water and is greeted with a mirage; for a sliced second, I doubt my senses. The white light flashes again; a second time, there's no sound to follow. It was the sign. I know I've found her. It was done—the SuperStar.

I've been navigating this borderless forest for three days now. When I don't dream of genies who can whisk the nightmares away, I dream of Carcine— my first love, my only love—the man who sacrificed his life for me, for the mission. I see him in my dreams. I feel his touch in the breeze. His memory gives me life. Without it, I feel lonely—one with the sun, but never satisfied. The rainbow, it seems, is not enough. So, I befriend the hanging moss, abiding in the shadows it casts. I run with the orange wildcats and soar with the bats. A city girl by birth, I was raised in the ravenous forest. Emerging by night, never by day; the night sky was my protection, the blackness my cloak. Although this streak of white burns a path to the golden field I've been hunting for these last few days, it also makes me a target for lurid bounty hunters hiding in the brush. They are bigger than I am, stronger than I am, but never smarter.

Nevertheless, I don't feel the cryptic heat of the bounty hunter searing my neck. I know the feeling all too well. I've eluded their venomous grip since age nine.

A SuperStar: Someone had become a star. A man who walked backwards and spun into infinity had instantaneously combusted into the ethos, so said the oracle. The planet would celebrate; cheers to them. It was the sign Ice told me to look for. As I slip between this tangle of branches and web of leaves to its edge, this nine-inch dagger hot on my thigh, I tip my White Sox hat over my brow (a nod to the SuperStar) and slice through the sea of yellow stalks like a blazing machete. I battle fear and anticipation like a ram bucking horns with a foe. It is the only way to conquer it. I pray no Tigers are behind me. As far as I know, I killed them all.

"I've never known peace. Frankly, I don't know what I've gotten myself into."

— Rayla Illmatic aka Red Feather. Dugon Rain Forest, MLK 09, 2212

"Find the Field of the Yellow Lady," Ice said; "and when the white light of the SuperStar hits, run like hell through it." Shakur Moulan would be on the other side. Shakur Moulan, whom no one had seen since the war began, was reportedly alive. Rumor had it that she escaped to Earth. One of the lucky few, we figured. But the space program was cut shortly before her disappearance, a program that ended largely because of her failures and The Missing Persons she couldn't explain. Now we're here, cut off from the Mother Planet and under the forced duress of The Dirk. We're trapped. But if Moulan is indeed alive, and Ice's statement that she was on "the other side" did indeed mean the land of the living, then a meeting could change the course of the war.

"I listen for the answer and hear nothing. My breath is the answer."
— Rayla Illmatic aka Heather Mack. Lost Count, Anywhere.

4

Ice, with all her wisdom, was as elusive as this war had become. Her guidance, while brilliant, was the proverbial knife in the pillow, as unsettling as it was comforting. But that's what spirit guides do, or so I've learned. Since she just appears to a few of us (those with "ears that see"), I've learned to trust that she's chosen us for a reason, part of which is to help. Although, her help mimics the path of no return, pushing me to the edge of my own reality in a crazed abyss, as I cling to answers without knowing the question. Faith, she called it. This was the life I lived, the life I've chosen, the path my father birthed me to live.

"I get it in."– Rayla Illmatic aka Scissor, In the Stars, Timeless. Moonwalker

Six miles through the Yellow Lady and counting: I'm treading lightly, the wheat still nipping my calves, but my breath is growing heavy. My speed is ebbing. Not too long ago, I could run 25 miles with ease; but a year of war-torn battles in short city alleyways made this run rougher than usual. How long is this field, I wonder? My bust heaves just above the field's horizon. I crouch lower, but I keep running. I would know when to stop, just like I know that the Dirk is waiting for me on the outskirts of Obama City, plotting my demise. They've been plotting for a long, long time.

I stop.

Ah, the roar of thunder.

"Nice."

Was that my inner voice? Was it Ice speaking? Were Carcine's whispers haunting me again? Or was it Moulan? The sky-high stalks glimmer under the new star. It's beautiful. Must have been quite the man, this SuperStar. But I've learned not to lose myself in the beauty of nature. One drifting thought equaled another casualty, another day away from the end of the war. That's when I saw him. He walked out of the night sky, his silhouette mapping a constellation. Black curly hair formed a halo over his indigo skin. He had a smoking stick dangling from his mouth. He was taller than I expected and stood as if he were waiting to be etched in stone. A rockstar of a warrior, I'd only heard about his victories, knowing one day we would meet. His glasses were black, but I could see myself in them.

"About time," he said in a warm, raspy voice. I knew this voice.

"You Delta Blue?" I asked, as my hand gripped the blade at my side.

His smile was the sun.

"Your troops are waiting, Princess."

Like geysers shooting out of a spring, an army of men and women sprang

5

from the thick of the yellow, sword and shield in hand.

I smiled, despite myself. No one had called me Princess in a long time.

Chapter 2

The Amness

I am Rayla Illmatic, citizen of Planet Hope, daughter of a new-age astronaut, chief strategist, and granddaughter of our Planet's first griot, Ice West. Few people know my name these days. I've been going under an alias since I was nine; when my father, Kent Illmatic, first of the new-age astronauts, led the premier protest against the Great Takeover, and the Dirk militia kidnapped him in the night, never to be seen again. He was the first to call me Princess; but I've gone by other names—Red Feather, Heather Mack. And when I strategized our rebel operations in the Dugon Rain Forest, and we recaptured Obama City, intuitive precision earned me the nickname Scissor.

I've been living in the shadows of Obama City, our base and capital, ever since the Great War began.

"Walk this Way ... Talk this Way." – Aerosmith

"I am the way and the light." – Yeshua

Planet Hope has been inhabited by earthlings for 200 years. As far as we know, no one else has ever lived here. Our planet was an experiment in the creation of a new society that Earth used as a model for achieving global peace. Earthlings had been scouring the galaxy, looking for another solar rock suitable for life for decades. The story goes that a genius kid astronomer, looking for Hailey's Comet, built some crazed telescope, which outpowered that of the space program. He stumbled upon a small planet, four planets from the newly discovered red sun, just a few galaxies away. And after much debate as to whether we were large enough to be an actual planet, the scientists of the time discovered that this "ribbon in the sky" was suitable for human life. Planet Hope is one-eighth the size of Earth, so the remaining digitablets say. But our mild temperatures, lakes, and grasslands are identical to Earth's. Though there are some differences: For one, our grass is blue, not green; our water purple, not blue. We have two moons, and we're littered with crystals. Our animals, like our people, are imported.

Earth sent some of their best minds—scientists, doctors, artists, educators, meta-physicians—each devising and implementing models to ensure peace and cooperative existence.

Planet Hope was built on the principle of universal love and cooperation. As achievements were made, Earth used these strategies to improve their own world. We high-kicked them out of the Information Age and into the Age of Intuits. We are credited with establishing the New Earth. Flying machines and vehicles that run on air-compression systems, solar-powered energy rings that powered everything from heating systems to home appliances, and a host of eco-friendly power sources emerged. We uncovered the "fountain of youth," a lifestyle and herbs that prevented aging. We cured all disease. Our technological advances were only rivaled by our models for human life. We devised a system without currency, an education program that reinvigorated learning, punishment without prisons, and a score of never-before-seen shifts in humanity. I hesitate to say "never before seen." According to Ice, there was a land called Atlantis and Lemuria that rivaled our blend of naturalistic and highly technological reasoning; but by the time the Planet Hope space project began, few with 20th century thinking knew it even existed.

The South Beach of the Milky Way – Pimp My Spaceshuttle

Accomplishments aside, we were fast becoming a hot spot for space tourism. Rich people, who could afford the astronomical cost of luxury along the Milky Way, ditched the tropical havens of their own planet and vacationed on Planet Hope. "Better than Mars, Closer to Heaven," the slogan cried. Vacationers came and didn't want to leave, some stealing away in hillsides and on islands, praying their families wouldn't force their return. Soon, many Earth people were clamoring to live on Planet Hope. To match the overwhelming demand, a lottery system was devised, and people from all corners of their world were sent, eager for a new life, a new beginning.

All was well at first. The cooperative living models on Planet Hope made the place a paradise for early citizens. It was a cultural golden age. Our architecture blended the best of Earth's antiquity and modern years with a distinct voice all our own. Crystal pyramids, with diamond domes and glass towers lined in gold, were the crowning glories of the cities. Pristine waterfalls and teepee rainbow dwellings were scattered throughout the land.

Earth, unable to resolve its bouts with crime and poverty, wanted to implement a galactic prison system and hold its undesirables on Planet Hope. It began under the guise of rehabilitation, and Planet Hope used its best social scientists to provide full-fledged programs for enlightenment—with incredible success. Quickly, it became clear that Earth planned to use our dear planet to be an all-out human dumping ground. They tried to ship inmates by the thousands. Our leaders refused to implement this space prison system and rallied for independence. The big governments of Earth agreed. We celebrated and called ourselves the Light Givers, citizens of Planet Hope.

"OMG—I'm a Planet Hoper." — lmao

After the Planet Hope rebellion, Earth decided to cut back on its space program. The costly Project Hope, despite its achievements, was deemed a failure. Earth was at risk of a serious brain drain and opted to keep flights to Planet Hope to a bare minimum. Trips to Earth were temporarily curtailed. We needed to focus on developing our own culture away from Earth, said experts. Although we maintained communication, citizens of Planet Hope opted to live completely self-sufficiently.

My grandmother, Ice West, was one of the first to come to Planet Hope. Her job was to catalog early planet history and ensure that the Light Givers knew where they came from. She created a library about Earth, its countries, people, wars, and achievements. She curated museums and launched an education program in our planet schools. But it was all so long ago, and once we declared independence, council leaders decided it was the future, and not the past, that we should focus on. A museum in her honor, celebrating her work, stands at the center of Red Sun City.

We were an interdependent community with incredible resources. We lived in peace for many decades. Then things began to change.

"Keep hope alive." – Rev. Jesse L. Jackson

The atmosphere on Planet Hope shifted. It was a slight shift, but radical enough to alter our hydrogen-powered vehicles. We couldn't drive. We couldn't fly. The team of busy scientists got to work. That's when Shakur Moulan, chief researcher and director of the Space Matters, unleashed her greatest program: The Teleport Project.

All of this energy-powered living was old school, she said. Why lug around in heavy vehicles when we could use our mind to go anywhere we wanted, she argued. The argument captured the imaginations of the heartland; and scientists, government, and citizens were championing this new age in transportation.

"I'm a third-generation glow stick." – Rayla Illmatic

Glowsticks and the rise of Merlin the Magician

Moulan, with her crack-the-whip personality and infectious giggle, was a second-generation Light Giver. The daughter of an educator and a physicist, she was sent back to earth for some specialized training no one could describe; and she returned with a power no one understood. While Planet Hope had a host of intuitives and spiritualists who worked with the science program, none could match her knowledge of the seen and unseen. No one had the mystic power of the mind like her. Others could back their theories with scientific knowledge. Moulan just seemed to know, and there was a force that enclosed her that brought things into existence. When our lakes went dry and the rainy season was low, she drew a picture of a winding stream, and instantly the lakes were filled. When the earth shook for the first time, lodging a 150-foot crater out east, Moulan reportedly went into some sort of trance state and the crater repaired itself instantly. Some said her words were laced with magic and that anyone in her reach would bend to her will. But the people of Planet Hope loved Moulan. Anything she wanted, we'd gladly do.

Your wish is my command.

Moulan set out to train several dozen people in her brand of study; my father was among them. With a bit of concentration, she reasoned that one could magically move from, say, their eating room to a friend's home several miles away, in a matter of milliseconds. The potential was exponential.

The team of trainees hit the ground running. I think I was seven years old when I, along with the entire population of schoolchildren, stood in the center of Obama City and witnessed a mile-high stack of marble disappear and then reappear a quarter mile up the road—all while my dad and his new friends focused their mind power to do so. We gasped with glee. Soon the distances that goods could travel grew longer, with the marble starting in one town and morphing in a town on the other side of our world.

The more talented of the bunch were able to transport themselves, hopping from city to city like global leapfrogs. My dad was the king of this, appearing and reappearing in all 18 cities on Planet Hope within 93 seconds. The kids in town called him Superman. But Dad said to just call him Illmatic, and kids emblazoned their shoes and tunics with his image and name. For fun, Dad and I would play hide and go seek in the fruit gardens near the house. While I would make the mango trees and nestled grape vines my spots of preference, Dad would pop from one tree to another, teasing me and taunting that I couldn't catch him. Government heads on Planet Hope even sent back word to Earth of our incredible discovery. Earth wanted to learn more.

Then Moulan, always one to up the ante, came up with the golden idea of teleport space travel. Forget these dated clunker rockets; let's teleport to other planets. Earth was our target. A team of 20 were selected and trained. My father was the first. He left MLK 28, 2192. I remember standing at the space center, along with a cheering throng of well-wishers, eager to watch the first intergalactic teleport. My dad, a man whose swagger and easy smile melted hearts, waved to the crowd, closed his eyes; and in a flash, he was gone. He returned three days later with amazing stories. He met with Earth's U.S. President and returned with substance to reinvigorate our drying lakes. Others went as well and returned with incredible tales of adventure. In fact, a few expeditions transported citizens (without the ability to transport on their own) to earth and back, much like the chosen few could transport cargo. The planet couldn't be happier.

But Moulan, never one to settle, came up with another idea. These solo missions and Earth-bound travel were great, she said, but let's create a team who can send crews of people to other planets. Let's be the leaders in space-age exploration, she declared. I remember watching the announcement on television with my babysitter Sui Lee. The crowd went wild, Moulan stood like a wizard in their midst; but Dad, whose smile was his trademark, wasn't smiling the same. In fact, I think he looked sad.

There were a couple of barriers the team would have to overcome: For one, much of this teleporting technique had to do with visioning. Literally, Dad and friends could only appear in places they were already familiar with. At the very least, they were given pictures of the targeted destination, which is why travel to Earth and other areas on Planet Hope were easier targets. Secondly, travel to other planets was complicated by the atmospheres that encompassed them. They simply weren't fit for humans. While some of these problems were circumvented with travel from Earth to Planet Hope, the possibility of going elsewhere seemed extremely difficult, despite our technological innovations. Some planets had temperatures so hot that a human's fragile body would instantly combust upon arrival. Others had gases so poisonous that no known spacesuit could protect them. The task was ambitious but wrought with complications. Yet Moulan, who seemed to have the answer to everything, came up with a solution that satisfied the Space Council, and she was allowed to proceed.

"I saaaiiiiddd your wish is my command. Now talk to the hand."

The new-age astronauts would create a mental force field so vast and intense around themselves that no gas, heat climate, or other terrain hazard could penetrate. Within this force field, they could carry all their needs, including food and oxygen. Collectively, they would study the telescopic pictures of the planet they were to land on; and collectively, they would have to envision the same thing. Three planets and a team of 100 were selected. They would envision a force field to protect themselves from the planetary atmosphere and, through visioning and the other techniques Moulan taught them, they would arrive on

11

each planet, gather information, and return. Mission One would last a week.

Again, Sui Lee and I went to the space station atop Mandela Mountain. We could barely hear ourselves above the crowd's screams and cheers. A guard let me ebb a little closer. I leaned onto the rail for a better view. The 100 men and women, my dad included, held hands in a giant circle. Moulan stood at the center. They chanted words I'd never heard, in a tone that was unfamiliar. They did this for what felt like hours, but Sui Lee said it was no more than 30 minutes. They raised their hands, looked to the sky, and vanished. A week went by. Day 8—we all returned to Mandela Mountain. It was the month of Gandhi, Day 18, Year 2193; we arrived at sunrise and waited. We waited until nightfall, and I fell asleep in Sui Lee's lap. The following day, I awoke, fearing I'd missed all the action. I hadn't missed anything. They hadn't returned.

Touch me in the morning, and then just walk away. – Diana Ross

For two months, crowds returned to Mandela Mountain and no one returned. Moulan explained that there were some time lapses in space travel; and, arguably, how we defined a week was not the same in other atmospheres. We'd all learned this in elementary school, so no one found Moulan's explanation comforting. The planet grew anxious. Scientists used their galactic telescopes to scour the planets where the astronauts were to arrive. But they found nothing. President Guatemala Che contacted Earth.

Earthlings reportedly looked everywhere in their world, from the highways of America's cities to the Sahara stretched across Africa. Submarines were sent into their waters; Moulan said that was ridiculous. The new-age astronauts weren't working with Earth's images, so there's no way they would have landed on the planet. But her memorable giggle hinted at nervousness. "Then where are they?" President Che demanded. Moulan said she, and we, had nothing to worry about. Because Moulan was always right, it was difficult not to believe her. President Che, whose sister and son were among the new-age astronauts, told us to pray.

And I did. Every night and every morning, I said the affirmations Dad taught me.

"I am one with the great one. I am one with life."

The revolution will not be televised ... the dictatorship will run on banner ads ...

1 million impressions and counting.

Hammer Dirk, President Che's chief council, pressed Moulan for answers. As the time grew on, Dirk convinced President Che to strip Moulan of her space station duties, assuming control himself. Dirk, a man more stout than he was short, was the policy wonk behind President Che's altruistic leadership. He was a well-respected man, the ultimate team player, and played the enforcer. Not everyone was in support of Dirk's latest actions. For one thing, he wasn't a scientist nor was he known for his mystical insights. While he'd taught in the Planet's universities, he wasn't known for teaching either. In fact, despite his heights in the government, it was hard to put a finger on just what Dirk's specialty was. Quiet, but with a knack for facilitating teamwork, he was a steady man whose chess moves were calculated 20 steps ahead. When citizens of Planet Hope thought of Dirk, people talked of his loyalty and devotion; his hard work and long hours; and his uncompromising stance to uphold all that Planet Hope stood for.

At the end of the day, we just wanted our families back. But Moulan's waning powers shook our stability. Her omniscience was all we knew. Dirk pledged to find The Missing, even if Moulan could not. Moulan, whom we'd once adored, slowly became the fixture of our anger and loss. As the weeks went by with no updates, our love commandments taught to everyone in the Planet schools were slowly etched away, and a campaign to isolate Moulan emerged. Dirk called her an enemy to our peaceful, loving ways. Dirk said she'd led efforts to undermine our Planet's mission. Many agreed. When Moulan refused to teach Dirk the teleporting skills, she was lambasted as a tyrant on the rise.

But all of this was circumstantial evidence. Most felt that the astronauts would return, eventually, even if it was wreaking havoc on the planetary consciousness. But something mysterious unfolded that no one could explain, then or since. Professor Kenyatta Mot was teaching his quantum physics class at the University of Yemoje, when, in the midst of explaining an equation, he vanished. Milt Plat, art teacher at the University of Demeter, vanished too, while presenting his latest work at the Nirvana City Festival. Audiences figured it was a joke, but when he didn't return, they panicked. A rash of disappearances followed—all high-profile citizens, all givers of light, all space program-affiliated. All eyes were on Moulan, who, in addition to being speechless as to the location of the astronauts, was even more confused by the rash of vanishings.

Then President Che disappeared. According to reports, she was meeting with cabinet members, signing new legislation for the children of The Missing, when suddenly she vanished. One witness said it was as if she faded slowly before their eyes. Panic swept the nation. Dirk called for volunteer guards from the ranks of the former inmates to set up camp at stations around the planet. We'd never had armed forces before. Dirk called them the Tigers; and, in addition to protecting the citizens, the Tigers were to capture Moulan on sight.

But I wasn't aware of most of this then; a young girl with a hearty doll collection and science lab. I would say my affirmations and chants, like Daddy taught, and all would be well. Sui Lee agreed.

13

"Stop moving at the speed of light, that's slow and so yesterday." – Rayla

Then one day while I was playing with my dolls at the foot of my pink-lit bed, my father suddenly appeared. He fell onto the white couch, exhausted. His eyes were lifeless. Only a glimmer in his eye indicated that he saw me. I was on the fringe of exploding with glee, but he put an index finger to his lip, begging my silence. I tiptoed his way, and he hugged me; a feeling engulfed me that I'd missed in his absence. He eased his embrace, slipping off the couch, and pulled the heavy curtains shut.

"Hide in the cupboard," he whispered. I obeyed, opening the tiny marble door where we kept *The Great Book* that Ice wrote. I slipped inside, stilling myself as I awaited my next instructions. I heard nothing. While I could breathe, I felt choked by the silence. I peeked through a crack, at one point, and saw my father standing by the window, peering through a slit. He was holding a weapon, the first time I'd ever seen one. Weapons were banned on Planet Hope. Ready for battle, maybe? Looking for someone? I dared not ask. When he saw me, the light streaming through the crack, he nodded (a simple instruction for me to shut the cupboard door and wait). I waited for what felt like eternity, pushed the door ever so slightly, but he was gone. He's in another room, I guessed. I shut it again. No noise. No sound. I would wait.

I was asleep when the cupboard door flung open, the white sunlight shattering my solace in blackness. Sui Lee snatched me into her arms, threw a fuzzy, purple blanket over my head, and flew out our crystal house. She carried me as fast as her long legs could take her; a gazelle, she dipped through alleyways and took to the Dugon Rain Forest.

My father was the only new-age astronaut who returned. Dirk, upon his arrival, had him captured. How a teleporter can be captured is a mystery to me. He was charged with launching war against Planet Hope, accused of facilitating The Missing, to instill fear and ultimately take over the planet. My father couldn't argue his case in the trial. They'd captured and reportedly killed him before it began.

That night in the Dugon Rain Forest, Sui Lee named me Red Feather and took me into the caves where the Stones were born. Dirk took over Planet Hope, destroyed our way of life and the peaceful cooperation we'd established. Fear, protesters reasoned, was no excuse for undermining the progress Planet Hope had made. Dirk ignored them. He cut off our supplies. He manned the schools. He ended our contact with Earth, dismantled the space station program and the Teleport Project, opened a galactic prison; and anyone who protested was imprisoned without trial. I've lived in rebellion ever since.

As a daughter of Illmatic, there's a price on my head. Each rotation we make around our Red Sun, the price goes up.

14

I'm on the other side of the Field of the Yellow Lady, now. Her thorny wheat shafts are swaying with the early morning breeze. I smell the salty food roasting by the crackling campfire, but I'm not hungry. This light, these smells, cause too much attention.

"You're safe here," Delta says, sitting beside me. He must be reading my mind. In my sleepiness, I'd forgotten to create a force field to protect myself from empaths and intuitives, a skill Ice guided me in, shortly after she appeared to me at the age of 15. But Delta was a friend, a kindred spirit, or so I hoped. Yet and still, defenses have their place; so I focused and surrounded myself with an energy field, anyway. Delta, I knew, would sense it; but a girl had to keep something to herself.

Delta Blue is a warrior's warrior. He hailed from Shogun City, the first city to resist Dirk's rule and the only one never to be occupied. Legend has it that their town sits atop a secret underground maze, one of Moulan's astronaut training grounds; and Delta, whose mother was a fellow astronaut, somehow learned the ways of the maze. The problem with Shogun City is that while no one can get in, no one can get out. Delta's battles to keep Dirk's Tigers away were the inspiration that kept the rebellion going. Carcine used to joke that he was some kind of a demigod, not that the two had ever met. His cockiness was as legendary as his victories, though. A fellow hunter himself, Delta knows the risks of campfires and smells. He feels my worry, despite myself, and hands me a hot metal bowl of red thick soup. "No one can track you because no one knows this place exists. It's protected. Relax … not that you know what that is."

"How can there be a land on this tiny planet that goes undetected?" I ask. I knew the planet's terrain well; its mountains and city streets were as intimate to me as my own hands. Carcine made sure I knew the planet's terrain. He drilled maps into my head and made sure the seasoned scouts took me along to master the lay of the land. I missed Carcine. Carcine was our mission leader—my best friend, my lover. The Tigers hunted him down on his quest for the Field of the Yellow Lady a few months back. Ice had come to him in a dream and showed him the path, he said. I begged him not to go.

"You have to believe," he told me. For his sake and my sanity, I did.

I cried for weeks when our soldiers found him in the Dugon Rain Forest.

Maybe that's why I'm here, to honor him. Peace sometimes felt secondary.

I keep a blue crystal chip he gave me, safely tucked in my knife holster. I rotated the octagon chip in my hand for solace. Delta Blue and his ever-watchful eyes noticed my slim fingers twiddling the stone about.

"My favorite color," he chimed. I ignored him.

With the exception of Shogun City and this place, I'd covered the world over. When Ice whispered the Field of the Yellow Lady to me, I questioned my sanity. I told my team I had to leave. They argued with me, but Ice's words were strong. Carcine's tug on my heart was strong, too. I'd be gone, I told them. But when I returned, I'd have the keys to the end of the war. They were heartbroken. Another one of the team sacrificing themselves for the whole. But my end would be different. I had their spirits to protect me; and I was smarter—smarter than Dad, Sui Lee, and yes, even Carcine. My intellect was my default when intuition and physical prowess waned. I prayed I was right.

I made it. Carcine didn't. No point in asking why.

No point in crying.

Delta continued to hover. I could feel the warmth from his body like I could feel my own heartbeat. I shivered. I don't want to look at him, wanting my own moment in this weird place. But Delta doesn't care. He whipped out a match and lit his stinky smoking stick, a fixture from the old world. I fan the smelly smoke. He drops it in the dirt and mashes it with his steel-toe boot. "It's one of many," he says, referring to our whereabouts. "Only the seers can enter," he says. The light-heartedness of the band of troops, their low laughter, and hearty pace annoy me. This place of peace in our war-torn world bothers me, too. "Relax," he said, an echo of himself. "Relax, while you can. And when you're ready, she's over there," he said, pointing to a tiny cottage with pink stone walls and brass door knocks.

But I was simmering, thinking of Carcine and wondering just what exactly Delta Blue knew. Clearly, he could have protected Carcine. Surely, he must have known he was coming, too.

He reaches for my hand. I pull away.

"How long have you been protecting her?" I asked, suddenly realizing that the storm of troops who greeted me were all under Moulan's command. My discomfort was justified. I dumped the red soup in the grass. A potion or a poison, I couldn't tell. Delta frowned. He was her protector, not mine. I inched away, staring into his dark glasses, hand on my blade. I stared hard. I could see his eyes.

"If it were all a trick, I would have never sent thought waves to find you."

"What does she want?"

"What we all want. Ice didn't tell you," he said, sneering.

"Tell me what?" I asked. How did he know Ice? Did she speak to him, too?

"Carcine didn't tell you?" he asked, his eyes narrowing.

My heartbeat quickened. This web of secrets; why was every road bent? I stood up, brushed the yellow field dust off my thighs, and headed for Moulan's cottage.

"You should eat first," he shouted. "She's not much of a cook. I'm much better," he said, flashing a grin.

"Whatever," I remarked, and marched off to Moulan's.

Chapter 3

The Westside of Dorothy's Rainbow

No need to grip the brass door knocks because the heavy white door squeaked open as I approached. I walked in cautiously, the door shutting behind me. From the outside, the stony cottage appeared to be no more than 12 by 12 meters, as I figured it. But inside, the looming palace and its mirrored walls were castle size. The entire place from rug to ceiling was a hue of green: emerald green, lime green, mint green, olive green, sea green, blue green. A winding staircase with six-inch porcelain figurines snaked down the wall to my right. An open library with shelves of multihued books, a relic of the old world, stood to my left. I stood in the guest room. But beyond its doors lay a seemingly infinite dark green vestibule with a myriad of golden doors. Above, a silver-rimmed balcony hovered. The place was so silent I could hear my own breathing. "Hello," I said. My voice echoed, as if I were standing in a cave. There was no reply. I circled the foyer, studying the odd figurines and gargoyles, and headed for the library. Racks of books were stacked on shelves as far as the eye could see. The bindings were heavy with rich embossing. I traced my fingers along the sleeves, walking the rows like a panther in trance. I'd seen books before, but never so many at once. A bright red one with gold stitching and a cross-like emblem caught my eye, and I popped it open. "You are the hero of your own story." I flipped through and stopped at a photo of a beautiful woman, a queen with some regal feather and gold headdress, seated on a throne. Her brown eyes locked with mine.

"Fascinating, isn't it?" Shakur Moulan said. Her sweet voice was jarring. And suddenly I was nervous. I whipped around, startled and guilty, holding the red book in my hand. Moulan smiled and descended down the staircase so gracefully she nearly floated. She's an attractive woman, petite in size; and her femininity was a site to behold in a world where gowns and parties were nonexistent. Her bevy of coiled black locks was twisted into an ornate bun. She wore a sea-green gown that cascaded at her ankles and pinned ever so tightly at the waist. A gold butterfly pendant rested on her bosom. She looked more like a good witch than a scientist, but nothing is ever what it seems.

I stood before her in war-torn wares: an ancient baseball cap, muddied ripped tee, and man boots soiled in blue dirt. I'd forgotten what it was like to be beautiful. "Shower?" she said, as if she were asking. I nodded and she pointed to a large door on the right.

What is this place? I wondered as the purple water cascaded down my back. The steam from the shower was so soothing; I could have lapped in its sweetness forever. The soap's grapefruit scent was hypnotizing. But I was on a mission. Sui Lee had mentioned a project where scientists were taking planet vortexes with high energy and creating virtual homes. I'd never thought much of it until now. Is this a virtual home? What other inventions has Moulan been working on? Has she been here all along? Did she know about our war? Did she care?

Yet, this shower in the pristine made my temper rise. She lived in this protected palace, while the rest of us barely survived.

A purple ensemble was folded neatly on a table outside the shower room along with a simple black bra, which in these times was impossible to find. The one-piece ensemble clung to my body, second to my own skin. Fortunately, the accompanying bronze tunic covered my curves, always a difficult task. I fastened a golden sash around my waist. My hair, still wet from the shower, was curling tightly. By nightfall, it would be full as the moon.

When I returned to the dining room, Moulan had set the table.

"Let's have tea," she squealed. She was a bit giddy for my taste, but I ran with it.

We sat at a square oak table. She poured a steamy batch of sweet tea for me in a vase-like goblet. She took her seat and held her goblet up for a toast. I abided.

"To the Rebellion," she said, nearly singing.

"To the Rebellion," I said. I wanted to begin my inquiry right away, but Moulan had questions of her own.

"They call you Princess. Are you an advocate of feudal society now?" she said, giggling.

"It's a term of affection," I say.

"Is it? And that dingy White Sox hat. I haven't seen one of those in ages. Why do you wear it? A tiara of some sort?"

"They were Earth gods. Ice wrote that the U.S. President wore one."

"Something like that?" she said. Her laugh was caught in her throat. She coughed.

"How's Sui Lee?"

"The Tigers captured her three rotations ago."

"Did they?" she asked, as if she didn't believe me. I chose not to respond.

"And the others? Your caravan of strategists and troops, do they plan to stay in the forest forever?"

"Some are in Obama City," I said. But I felt that Moulan knew the answers to these questions. I guess it's all a part of some formality she rarely had the chance to enjoy.

"You'd be surprised at what I don't know," she said, taking another sip of her tea.

"We thought you were on Earth."

"So did I," she said, laughing so hysterically, I wondered if I'd missed the joke. She guzzled down another dose of tea.

"I love Delta Blue. Don't you?" she said, giggling again.

"Never mind me; I just don't get to have much girl talk. Everyone's so damned serious these days. I'm glad you're here. I've been waiting for you."

"I want to talk about the space program," I interjected. "What happened with the teleport sys—"

"Oh, I know why you're here. Do we have to talk business now?" she asked, her sea-green eyes pleading.

I nodded.

"I need to learn how to teleport. It's the only way we can save Planet Hope."

"Is that so?" she said, sucking the tea through her teeth. "And they call you a strategist. Funny—is that your one trick? Your magic bullet theory to save

20

poor Planet Hope," she asked coyly. "Do you have a better idea?" I asked. "Surely, you've been doing more in this fairy-tale world of yours than whipping up batches of tea," I said.

Moulan snorted.

"Joke's on you, Cupcake," Moulan said, her eyes narrowing with mischievousness. "Follow me," she said, pushing away from the table and gliding to the library.

"Respect yourself." – Madonna Ciconne, US, 1987

"I was born this way." – Lady Gaga, US, 2010

"Over 200 years have passed since humans began space travel," Moulan said, nestled in her comfy velvet chair. "We have telescopes that can find other galaxies, and yet we've never found any tangible proof that life exists beyond Earth and Planet Hope. Does that strike you as odd? Think about it; we've scoured the universe with our satellites and missions, but not one sign of life anywhere? This vast, infinite universe is lifeless? How could that be?"

"Ice said that Earthlings used to report UFO sightings," I stated. But Moulan ignored me. She sauntered toward the rows and rows of books. I followed her.

"Illmatic was the first to figure it out. He was a student of time. Time, the one thing in human mind that exists nowhere else but on this three-dimensional plane. Time, why would we ever itemize the infinite?" she said sighing.

"It defines our experience," I said. She snapped around.

"Do you need to know what time it is to know who you are?"

I wasn't sure what she was leading to. I didn't respond. But I was beginning to feel light, almost like I was floating, suspended perhaps between this Moulan world and my own.

"Teleporting was never the problem," said Moulan, dragging her fingers along the binding of the books. "We do variations of it all the time, a daydream, a dream, a fantasy. Do you ever have any fantasies?" she asked.

"Yeah, but you're just traveling in your mind."

"Precisely. You catch on fast. "

I was confused.

"Humankind has always been obsessed with the great beyond. But what's out there is really in here," she said, clutching her hand to her breast. Outer space is inner space."

My knees buckled slightly. Had I been poisoned?

"You have not been poisoned," she snapped, reading my thoughts. She placed her tiny hand under my chin and lifted it. Our eyes were aligned.

"Hear me, Little Muffin, and hear me well. There is no Planet Kiso. There's no Mars, no Venus, no Planet X—nothing, not in this time, anyway. Those planets are repositories for our other lifetimes." She walked off, and I followed.

"So when we look in the telescope and see other planets, what are we looking at?" I asked. The faster she talked, the faster she walked, and I was nearly jogging to keep up with her. I glanced down at the lacy hem of her gown, some six inches above the ground. Wait a minute; she really is floating.

"Projections—portals for other aspects of the soul," she said cavalierly. "All these other planets are imagined spaces in our subconscious; there is in reality only us. Therefore, if you call yourself going to another planet, there is no other planet to go to. You can only go to another dimension in your mind, another place in your subconscious—another lifetime." She stopped in her tracks, turning about; and I nearly collided into her. "And that's where The Missing are stuck, in another lifetime, another place, another field where they've lived a life as someone else. Or they're in some future life. But because time is infinite, and our souls are expansive, one can't place where in human history they could be. Moreover, once they're there, they have no conscious memory of this life. No trigger to make them remember and teleport back."

"When the astronauts landed on what we thought was Planet Kiso, they entered another plane, some window to former or future life?" I asked.

"Illmatic figured it out. He was the only one who returned. He alerted me right away, and then he vanished." Moulan's eyes welled with tears. She wiped them away hastily.

"This world you've created is a portal to find The Missing," I said.

She nodded.

"I'm the Guardian of The Akashic Library," she said. "Every memory of every person who has ever lived is lodged here. Every answer to every question is here. I've been digging through these texts looking for clues. I'm close," she said.

"How do you know?" I asked.

"Because you arrived."

I stumbled, gasping for air. Moulan looked steadily.

"You should have eaten the soup. It makes these trips easier," she retorted. But I collapsed before I could respond.

Chapter 4

Don't Wake Me

YOU know how some people take naps and dream? Well, I take naps in my dream. Bizarre isn't it? I need the rest, I figure, using this dream to find the peace that escapes me in life. All the twisted caverns I plod through in dream world always lead to the same courtyard, where finally, after what feels like lifetimes of maze surfing, I find peace in a courtyard at the heart of a green garden paradise. I curl up on my side, the marble floor as my mat, and in the time it takes my eyes to scan the horizon, my lids grow so heavy that I fall asleep—in the dream, that is. But this night, instead of juggernauting to a new crazed adventure, I take a nap and then awake, still in the dream of course. I awake and the marble floor is so cold on my face, I feel like I'm on a block of ice. Both ends of the hallway are pitch black; I rise abruptly, pacing myself as I head toward a looming North door. The blackness swallows me, but before I can cower to fear, I see a light. A glowing, blue octagon crystal is lodged in a tree stump. The light glimmers just enough for me to realize I'm in a cave. But the crystal draws me. I'm pulled toward it, and I feel an energy rip through my chest. I arch my back, taking in the sheer power and force of the radiant light that feels as close to me as my own breath. And in a flash, I'm transformed. I'm no longer the Rayla I know, but rather some super being. I run to the cave's perimeter, climb narrow steps, and walk through a short door. The sun is so bright; I can't see anything but its bouncing rays. My eyes adjust and I'm startled by the sight of soldiers, dozens of them, on either side of me, lining the peninsula that peaks above a great ocean. I can taste the salt in the air, and the soft crash of the waves against the steamy sand calms me. This is my life. I see a large ship docked. A man I know, a king maybe, walks toward me. He's handsome, his sparkling eyes gleaming like the rays off his metal armor. I greet him. I know him. Is this Carcine? As we walk back together into the cave and down the hallway I emerged from, just seconds away from the curious soldiers, we embrace.

Then I awake – for real.

I'm balled up on a hard wooden floor. I don't know this room. Although in the dream I'm awash with homecoming, here I'm just at a loss for words. A hand brushes my shoulder; I roll around to face Moulan. She smiles sweetly and hands me a cup of orange tea. I douse it all down in one gulp, grab a neighboring pink pillow, clutching it as I press my back against the cool cobblestone wall.

Moulan wants me to find The Missing. Both Moulan and Delta Blue claimed that Ice said I would be the one; something she, in her twisted sense of humor, didn't manage to tell me.

But I don't want to do it.

I don't have time to find The Missing. I need to get to Earth immediately, rally some of their leaders, and bring in forces who can help us restore peace on Planet Hope. We hadn't had contact with Earth in so long, who knew what state their world was in. But I had a better chance of galvanizing their leaders than I did trekking through time looking for The Missing. If there were ships to fly, I would.

"But there are no ships. All you have is me," said Moulan, reading my thoughts. For the first time, her giggles slowed and a sadness flashed in her eyes.

"If I leave, I'll be lost forever," I said. "There's no guarantee I'll get anywhere; and, if I do, it will be in another time, another age. I could be a slave during the Roman Empire, a B-girl in 20th century America, a Geisha girl in China. I'll never remember who I am to get back, and even if I do, who would believe me? If I get there before the space age, they'll burn me at the stake. If I get there after the space age, I won't have the technology to get back, even if I wanted to."

But even if I skipped The Missing quest and went to modern-day earth, who's to say they'd come along? What am I going to do, teach them to teleport, they get lost, and then what? There are too many factors.

"Why don't you go?" I asked.

"This isn't about me," she said. "I know why I'm here. You, on the other hand, have something to prove, Princess."

I didn't like Moulan's steady self-assurance, this knowing without knowing that she's perfected so much. Moulan knew I couldn't say no to a challenge. I was the storm, but I was skeptical. She wasn't telling me something. I got the feeling she never would.

But I was weary of hiding and fighting. I wanted an end to the war and to restore possibility on Planet Hope. I longed for Dirk's rule to be over. I was so far from normal.

"If The Missing returned, the war would be over?" I asked.

She nodded.

"I know where they are," she said.

Now we're talking, I thought.

"But, you can't go alone. If it's going to work, you'll need to make a pact, some bond with a kindred spirit, a person who believes and harbors your same mission. It will keep you focused," she said.

My chest grew tight. Carcine was that one. He would go on the mission with me. Carcine was the reason I'd become the warrior I am today. He taught me everything he knew. He believed in me. Despite the teams who've backed me, I've felt the weight of battling alone. He was my soul mate, if there was such a thing. I would love to travel this journey with him. I wonder if that person needed to be alive in this world? Did my pact have to be amongst the living? In this time spectrum continuance in which there was no death, I knew that it very well could.

"You'll go with Delta Blue," she snapped, sensing my reasoning.

"Can't I pick my partner?"

"You already did."

Chapter 5

Cyber Sails in Juvember

MOULAN had it all figured out. I and Delta Blue would go to an East African kingdom in the 12th Century. According to her research, three of The Missing—Enuk , Anna, and Scotch—were biding their time as servants in the King's palace. All three navigated their way up the slave ranks to become trusted forces within the palace. Enuk's name was Fajah in this life. The wiser of the three, he had worked his way up to advisor, breaking from the slave ranks with his incredible dream interpretations. Anna, the fortune teller, was handmaiden in the palace. She had retained the same name in this life and the last.

"How is that possible?" I asked Moulan.

"Choice," she quipped.

As for Scotch, his name would be Malik. A bullish muscle man and smart talker, he was a top guy in the military and royal guard. All three were clairvoyant. They could see the future. Neither were any wiser to their previous life, each now stuck in their old identities. On Planet Hope, Enuk, Anna, and Scotch were second in command after my father. In their African life, they shared the gift of clairvoyance, a skill they were known for on Planet Hope. Moulan figured they'd be the easiest to convince and were the three most critical to the teleport project. Once they realized who they were, it was simply a matter of getting them all together, visualizing Planet Hope's Mandela Mountain, and in an instant they'd be home. Easier said than done, but it was all we had to go on. Fortunately, there was a mountain in the region, an exact replica of Mandela Mountain, which Moulan instructed us to run to, once we "remembered." The sight of this mountain would trigger the memory, and we'd be back home.

"What happens when we bring them back?" I asked.

"Let me handle that," said Moulan. "You just get them here."

Delta Blue and I had also lived some other life at this time, but Moulan wouldn't say who we were. "Better to discover yourself," she said. Moulan reasoned that because Delta and I were sent with a purpose, in a pact, that we would have a desire to complete our mission, even if we were just barely conscious of what that mission was. "You'll know even when you don't know," she said. We would recognize one another in several ways: For one, we would have the same birthmark, a shared mole on our right shoulder. Two, we would both have the same passion, an intense interest in space travel, an interest so unique and bizarre that we would instantly gravitate to one another. Three, we were to carry a small golden pendant, an embossed staff with a snake wrapped around it. Our longing for the night sky would remind us of Planet Hope.

"You'll share a secret," she said.

"What's the secret?" Delta asked.

"You tell me," she said, mired in her own giggles.

Delta and I looked at one another and shrugged. Like everything else, we'd know when we were ready to know.

These were all guideposts she said, guideposts to help us remember when we forget. Delta and I went through the training, an intense series of dream exercises.

After one session, Moulan called me into her parlor. I joined her at the table. A plate of carob brownies sat between us.

"You asked me why I'm not going," Moulan said.

I nodded, not really expecting Moulan to ever answer. Apparently, I was wrong.

"Nostalgia and regret is such a joy snatcher," she said. "You're lucky, you don't have any regrets, but I do."

Did she regret the teleport project, I wondered.

"I was in love with a man once, but we never made time for one another. We had a cause to fight, work to do, a mission to accomplish," she said, her eyes widening. "That man is out there or in here; and I know that if I see him in another life, and I have an opportunity to right our wrongs, I'll never come back," she said.

I swallowed hard.

"You have to release your attachments, Rayla. "

"I have," I said.

"I feel him in you," she said. "You can't let your love for Carcine compromise this mission. He made his choice. Now you must make yours."

"What do you mean 'he made his choice'?" I asked.

"Oh, Rayla, everyone has their own experience to live. It's a hard lesson, but a truthful one. He did what he had to do for him," she said.

"And what was that? And how do you know Carcine?" I asked.

Moulan slid the plate of brownies my way.

"Die daily and you'll live forever," she said, pushing herself away from the table. She glided out the door.

Chapter 6

Pirouettes in Silver Slippers When They Aren't Ruby Red

IN the heat of the training, Delta and I didn't talk to one another much. We were soldiers who shared a yearning to save our home, Planet Hope. He avoided my eyes when I looked his way. He would be leaving all he knew behind, risking life and limb. We would be partners. But I knew little about Delta—whom did he love? What would he miss? And his smoky glasses prevented me from seeing more. He was a man who knew missions and executed them. Personal ties were always trumped by duty to a greater cause. But even this mission was a hard pill to swallow and beyond the normal do or die sacrifice we'd grown accustomed to. The night before, I saw him talking to a tall female soldier with short red hair, under a great oak. They talked at length, and she was visibly upset. I felt a streak of guilt zip through my chest. In these final days, he should be spending these last few hours on Planet Hope with her, not me. All's not fair in love and war.

The night was poked with stars, and I spotted Delta at the edge of the Field of the Yellow Lady, looking to our three crescent moons. I joined him.

"They only have one of those on Earth," I said.

"They don't know what they're missing," he said, and tossed a rock in his hand over the horizon. "Nothing but war this way, anyway."

"But it is home," I said.

"Home is where you make it. We chose this life, Princess. Regret will just stifle that sunny enthusiasm of yours."

I don't remember choosing anything. But the greatest sin of man is forgetfulness, a notion that took on new meaning in this altered space time continuum.

"Tell me about Shogun City," I said.

"It would just screw up the mission; get you thinking about a place you can't go to, anyway," he said. "But when we return, I'll take you there, if you let me," he said.

"Is that—oh, what do they call it—a date?" I asked. Sui Lee told me about dating. In times of peace, lovers went to decorated places that served pretty food, listened to musicians, or watched people in odd costumes act out stories that made you laugh and cry. Sui Lee said that she and my dad used to go to a place called the movies, where they watched "films." Dirk banned the arts shortly after his takeover, and any media was government-controlled. Those found with films or unlicensed digitablets and unapproved information would be imprisoned. With such rigid controls, any information not funneled through the government-monitored system was used for communication amongst the rebels. Eventually, we abandoned the airwaves altogether and relied on mind power. It was safer.

But I did see a film once. Carcine and I were on a mission on the outskirts of Obama City. We were raiding a warehouse for food, and we stumbled into an empty auditorium with rows of chairs and a screen the size of a house. We headed to the top of the row and broke into a room filled with boxes of popcorn kernels. We were grabbing stashes when Carcine flung his arms around me and kissed me. He hoisted me up and my hips knocked something. Suddenly, a flashing image of a woman and some monster of some sort were dancing down a yellow brick road. They sang and danced (another banned activity). Music—I hadn't heard it in so long. Some of us rebels sang and danced in the forest or in an underground fortress in Obama City. But these two looked so free. Carcine and I both stood frozen, our eyes glued to the flickering image of this twosome easing down a road. They had plenty of theaters in Shogun City, or so I'd heard.

"You could get me in?" I asked, knowing Shogun City's deadbolt rules against the foreign-born. This fortress of a city was a utopia the foreign-born could only dream about. They were the inspiration for all the rebel forces. Shogun City was the one spot on the planet that maintained the original principles of Planet Hope. But I was toying with Delta Blue. If anyone could crack Shogun City's code of conduct, it was me. I just hadn't put my mind to it yet.

"Shogun City has a weakness for pretty girls. And if you bring back The Missing, they'll give you the key to the city," he said. "Maybe build a pyramid in your honor," he joked.

Part of the Shogun City royal guard, he was highly trained and very skilled in the art of war. His nuance for battle and analysis convinced me that he's done this before. I wondered if he was a soldier in the lifetime we were returning to. What was Carcine in another life? Who was I?

With this training overload, I didn't have time to contemplate any of it, fearing I'd stray if I gave it too much thought.

While I was totally unnerved about his trip to the great beyond, I kind of dug the idea of losing myself and living another life in another world—like that lady dancing around on that golden road in the "movie." In an odd way, it would be a pleasant escape from this planet we were trapped on, a nice breather from this way of life. By the looks of it, I'd be hanging around a palace. Although I'd be on a mission; for a moment, I could breathe. For a moment, I could live.

Maybe I'd go on a "date."

I'd be free. I felt my throat constrict. Freedom? What was that like?

I clasped Delta Blue's hand in mine. "Promise that you'll make sure I get back," I said. Delta Blue's eyes narrowed. He kissed my cheek. I'd never felt lips so soft.

"Promise that you'll come with me," he replied.

He wrapped his arms around me in reassurance, and we held one another in the tri-moonlight.

"I don't know what's up with Moulan and her moles and stargazing as bonding agents. If I remember anything, it will be your eyes. He removed his glasses. I saw his eyes, a hazy light brown, for the first time. "The only vulnerability you display are in those brown eyes."

"I'll always protect you," he said.

He kissed me. I didn't resist. His lips told the story. Delta and I had no connection, just two parents lost in an abyss and a killer instinct for surviving under Dirk's tyranny. We needed something deeper, something more committed to forge the bond we needed to survive space and time—a soul connection, a physical bone. We made love like there was no tomorrow; because for us the life we knew would temporarily be a distant one, one we longed for, more real in our dreams than our reality, until that one moment when it all clicked and we returned home. We made love like there was no tomorrow, because for us, there was none.

***

Delta and I lay side by side, wrapped like mummies in sheets on cold iron flatbeds. A giant lamp hung low and swayed gently like a pendulum. We were in Moulan's special teleport chamber. The silver room was clinical compared to the lush extravagance in the rest of the house. My eyes scanned the room. I could hear my own heartbeat. I could feel Delta's heart in mine.

"Close them," Moulan instructed. And we did.

The sonic gong was running vibrations through our bodies. I thought of Sui Lee running with me in the forest. I thought of Carcine guiding my hand, as he taught me the ways of the dagger. I thought of the Tiger, one of Dirk's forces, lunging at me in the Dugon Rain Forest, my blade piercing his side. I cracked his neck as he fell. I thought of Delta kissing me last night.

"Focus," Moulan said. I shivered. "See the mountain," Moulan instructed.

I envisioned Mandela Mountain, Illmatic, and The Missing chanting in a circle. The image morphed into me on Mandela Mountain alone.

I held on to the vision of me on Mandela Mountain. I felt the warm sun pierce my forehead. A bead of sweat fell from my temple. I felt the snake and staff pendant hanging from my neck. It was hot now, burning into my chest. This pendant would bind Delta Blue and I for life. I could still feel Delta's passion from the night before. The intensity freed me beyond my own self-recognition, and I needed an anchor, something I knew to trust in. Moulan was unaware, but I'd slipped the blue octagon crystal in the clutch of the pendant, too. Carcine would be with me always. To lose him was to lose myself. I needed him on this journey. I loved him. To forget him, was to forget me; and last night, I'd forgotten him. I'd betrayed his trust. A tear fell from my eyes. I felt a kiss on my forehead. Then it all went black.

Chapter 7

The Last Day of the Beginning of a Princess Life

"One day our people would become one with the source, our leaders would as-cend, and the reign of human limitation would be no more."

– Princess Rayla, 1132 AD,

THE sun is shining so brightly, I couldn't stay asleep if I tried. I push myself off the cool marble floor. The hall is empty. I must have fallen asleep. I've taken to naps on the floor. My father used to chastise me when I did it. "You are not a servant," he used to say, grimacing to hide his bellowed chuckle. But I get such a thrill from doing what everyone thinks I shouldn't be doing. I like napping like the cats. I disobey just for the fun of it.

"Princess, Princess," a small but loud woman, her head wrapped in white cotton, shrieks as she helps me stand. Her name is Anna—a peculiar lady with a long, golden braid down her back; my father bought her from a band of Persian merchants who'd found her somewhere far north. She was a fortune teller. My father took to her, and she was assigned to care for me in the palace.

"He's here," she says.

"Who?"

But Anna pulls me off the floor, dusting me off as she rushes me to a door. She waves her hand, flicking it like a wet rag, telling me to go forward. I walk

34

in the dark cavern of light, to my prayer crystal, a fist-sized green crystal embedded in a tree trunk. I stand before it, say my prayers, and my heart expands. An energy fills me so completely, I gasp in ecstasy; and then I run, holding my skirt, up the tiny winding steps to the exit. I step outside, and the sun is so bright, I can hardly see. I cup my hands over my eyes. Soldiers align the plateau, and a ship is docked. Hasaan is here to see me.

My head is spinning. My trusted heads of battle, Chaga and Malik, stand on either side. Chaga's hazel eyes are avoiding me. Memories from our night together last night hang like a wadded thickness between us. We sat together on the Cliff of No Return and stargazed. A shooting star scorched the sky, flung from one side to the next, like a cake saucer tossed across a room—like the sky ships I dream about. Chaga, my personal royal guard, stands poised as always. He knows how this works. Malik, head of the royal guards, feels the tension. He mumbles something, but I don't hear. I snap his way, and he lifts his chin, as if he's said nothing. Hasaan climbs up the winding stone steps, his team of men behind him. He presents me with a fist-sized turquoise crystal. I nod in appreciation. In a matter of days, he'll be my husband. He'll be the new King of Ku.

My life is just beginning.

No one approves of this alliance. Father died a short time ago. I'm his only daughter, and every king and chief within three days' walk is vying for my affection. Aasin, a gold-dripped Sultan from a neighboring city-state, with the largest harem in the region, came riding in with a bevy of decorated camels and giant elephants. Dropping coins along the way to the palace, some said he lowered inflation with the gold coins and nuggets he dropped in the hands of every peasant and traveler in sight. He didn't so much as ask for me, but requested a meeting with Fajah, asking if I would be his bride; as if I would actually consider living with a swarm of jealous women and their screaming kids and eunuchs. Fajah actually considered it. I refused and had to convince him to say no. And for that, I will never listen to Fajah again.

Others from across the great ocean bid for my affection, too. Our rich coastal trade lured a bevy of savvy merchants, ambitious seamen, and conquest-seeking royalty; many seeking a wife on this side of the ocean, as they bided their time waiting months for the winds to carry their ships back east. Sea-born queens were left alone for whole seasons at a time, standing by the ocean's shore, looking for their lovers to return with the changing sway of the wind. So when Raj, a prince from an island in the East, docked his boat—full of blue-dyed silks, ivory, and china—on my shore, claiming to have heard tales of my beauty (his so-called reason for making me his "wife on the sea"), I said no to him, too. I'm not much for waiting.

I soon became known as Princess No, a running joke in the region. Everyone faulted Father for not promising me to someone on his deathbed. No woman in recent history had ever had the power to say no to a wedding promise. They'll write about this in the sacred scrolls, I'm sure.

But the quest for a princess heart was not always amusing, a lesson I learned from Notia, my best friend—my only princess friend.

Notia, the daughter of a powerful family just south of our land, was the first and only princess allowed to be my childhood friend. We played together as girls; and of all the young women of promise in the region, she and I were the most valuable, a fact both of our families treasured and feared. Our shared hope and privilege was our bond, our isolation our fate.

Wars were fought over attractive princesses, and families of note were quick to take all precautions to protect us from the larger world. We were hidden gems, surrounded by well-intentioned advisors, guards, and guides, who smothered us with detailed attention. A fortress of pleasure. Notia was my only friend on the outside and my only contact with the larger world. A sunny girl who laughed a lot, we were the same age. She liked playing tricks on the guards and fooling the maidens who looked after us. When we were together, we talked about life beyond the courtyard.

"I want to ride one of the great merchant ships," she'd say.

"I want to ride a ship in the stars," I responded.

"Silly girl, there are no ships in the stars," she'd say.

"But maybe when we become queens there will be one," I added.

We danced in the gardens, we frolicked around the sacred scrolls, and Anna would take us out to the ocean and let us dance along the coastline with the drummers and pipe players. The townspeople and visiting merchants would cheer us on. As we grew older, Notia itched with restlessness; she became notorious for sneaking out of the palace late at night and flirting with the traveling merchants and pirates who camped out off the shore. During one of these escapades, she embarked on a lurid love affair with Lyo, a syrup-talking Swahili merchant, closer to the interior, who specialized in tanchara, or the gold nugget trade.

"I'm in love," she gushed, sticking a four-petaled pink flower in her thick braided hair. Anna had left us alone together in the courtyard garden, and we drank cups of mango juice with a lunch of alligator meat, lamb, and yams prepared by Notia's cook.

"You're in trouble," I replied. Although her tales were eye-popping treats, the danger of it snaked through her words like a cobra prepped to pounce.

Naturally, it didn't take long for news of Notia's nighttime adventures to reach her mother. Queen Akba was horrified. While she typically ignored her daughter's antics, this one risked the survival of the kingdom. Queen Akba's husband had passed away. Not trusting her own military, and fearing raids from the interior, she plotted to corner the all-things-blue market; and she had been meeting with Tzo, a leading sea captain from the Far East. The color blue, both rich in water and nighttime sky, is all but impossible to create in this region. And the people of our coast fell in love with the sky-colored silks, rugs, and china that the sea-faring men brought across the ocean. Queen Akba, in a rush to judgment, promised Notia to Tzo. But the alliance just angered the surrounding kingdoms, including my father, Chand, who had his own Far East connections. Lyo, who handled a significant portion of Queen Akba's gold trade, was killed by the Queen's men. While this pleased Tzo, the murder led to surrounding nations sanctioning Queen Akba's people, refusing to trade with them; and Tzo was banned from the coast. When Tzo returned at the turn of the wind to wed Notia, men from the surrounding kingdoms met him in the water and set his ship ablaze. Queen Akba's kingdom was raided. Notia, their proudest possession, was kidnapped in the raid. Some say Queen Akba bartered her prized daughter to attackers in exchange for peace. No one knew for sure; and in time, no one in the palace spoke of her again. But I remembered. My hope was that she is riding on a big ark in the sea. I thought of her fate often; when I was allowed to be alone, I cried.

When Notia disappeared, father assigned Chaga to be my personal guard. He was promised to me for life.

These men talk of my ravishing beauty or their adoration for my father, Chand; in truth, they know as well as I that they want this territory, fruit-rich land, our access to the sea, and our reputable repository of wealth in gold and secrets. Our self-contained land has need for little else but luxuries. Vegetation is plentiful. We eat from the land and sea; we drink from the fresh water lake we've filtered. Our builders have mastered masonry of seashell walls and bricklaying; our schools attract the promising ones in the region. I'm a prized capture and symbol of regional conquest. Hasaan is the only one of royal birth who wants me for me.

The peninsula is long and Hasaan's steps are diligent and forward. He's strikingly handsome. He is tall, a head and a half or so taller than I. His body is lean, chiseled with a narrow waist and solid legs. He's the image of the stone paintings that the ancients loved. His cheekbones are high; his dark brown eyes sparkle. I like the way he looks. I like the honey sway of his voice.

He's not the most powerful in the region, a fact that both Chaga and Fajah are quick to mention. Fajah, my father's advisor, was once a slave whose predictions for the future elevated him to one of the more powerful men in the court. He was my father's most trusted confidant, enjoying both the envy and love of others who viewed Fajah with suspicion. A rotund man with thick black eyebrows and a solid belly, Fajah didn't care much for matters of the heart. Chaga, on the other hand, was all too concerned about them.

Chaga was in love with me. While I cared about him, too, our affection didn't have a place in this world. In this world, my well-being and that of my people are chained to my ability to marry royalty with the right alliances; a reality that Chaga, a soldier and gifted poet, knew before he presented me with a gift, a gold and emerald snake and staff twin necklace he bought when he was on a trip with the Nubians. He has one. I have the other. Our affection was a secret that Fajah and Anna had caught wind of. I'm sure Chaga turned to Malik to confide in; thus his irritating frowns as Hasaan marched up the peninsula.

I tried to think of none of this, as Hasaan walked toward me. I greeted him with a smile, which he returned. We walked alone to my wing of the palace. Hasaan followed me into my room, my world in a box paradise. Blood-red rugs from the Persians flanked the marble floor. White cotton from the Egyptians adorned my bed; as well as golden lamps from the Arab traders; porcelain from the East; silver crosses from the people of Askum; jewelry from the Nubians; colorful red, green, and white stones from the people of the interior; sea-inspired gifts from the Manchinga, Mtakata, Miranga, and the many Swahili peoples who dotted the coast. I, too, loved all things blue and flanked the space with as many indigo-dyed silks and cotton as could be flanked across a room of this size. But my favorite was a double-edged iron sword that Hasaan had his best iron workers make, especially for me, with iron from Askum. It was the gift that stole my heart; the gift that offended Chaga, enraged Fajah, and made Anna gasp; the gift that compelled me to open my heart to this man who knew the land and sea.

Finally, away from the peering eyes, Hasaan wrapped his arms around me, our lips met, and he held me so closely I could feel his heart beating. I slid my fingers along his shoulder. His shoulder raised slightly; I saw a glint of metal in the corner of my eye, snatched the sword from the sheath against the wall, whirled away from him, and our blades crashed.

"What are you doing?" I shouted.

He didn't respond, swiping his sword left, then right, mine meeting his accordingly. I picked up my skirt with my left hand, swinging my right to block his every blow. My eyes were on his wrist, not his eyes, and this friend was now my enemy. I leaped over the bed, my back nearly thudding into the wall. He lunged my way; I dipped to the side. His sword was stuck in the velvet wall. Mine was at his throat.

"Good job," he said, knocking my blade leftward with his arm and pulling me in for a kiss. I pushed him off of me.

"I hate you," I retorted.

"But look how much you've learned," he said laughing. "You must have been practicing."

He fell into the bed and grabbed a green fruit from a basket on the table. I was winded. I hopped in the bed, stretched my arm across him, and lay beside him. I kissed the mole on his shoulder. He had one on his right shoulder, just as I did. It reminded me of Chaga.

"If you're going to lead a people, you have to be ready for battle. You can't look to me to do it all the time. And never let your guard down."

"Even with you?" I asked, rubbing my sore shoulder. He brushed my hand aside and massaged it for me.

"Especially with me." He nuzzled my neck and continued digging his fingers into my shoulder blade.

It's this odd teaching that Hasaan insisted on sharing—one in which I was as capable as he or any king, sultan, or chief; one that I delighted in and found as puzzling as it was empowering. The laws of my people, and his, didn't have room for warrior women; and yet Hasaan was intent on ensuring that I knew the ways of the chiefs, kings, and sultans. He was more committed to it than my own father, who left my protection in the hands of trusted assistants, but never me. It's this private teaching that made our moments together more magical than anything that Chaga could write or Fajah could say. They didn't know what we were doing when we were alone, assuming that we were making love only and being the subject of the city's latest gossip. But I didn't care. They didn't know about these magical lessons, and I didn't care to tell them. In fact, Hasaan discouraged it.

"Maybe I'll be the first woman sultan with a harem of men."

"How's that any different from what you have now," he said, laughing.

***

Our tribe was a puzzling bunch. The oracle said that we arrived on the Great Horn over a thousand years ago, after the Fire of the Gods destroyed our homeland. We trekked along the Nile through Upper Egypt, the land of the Nubians, to what would become home to the people of the coast. We were protected from the mainland by the mountains, whose height and depth warded off the storms of the sea. Despite the centuries we'd spent in the region, our neighbors considered us to be foreigners. Our ways were different. We took on the names and costuming of many peoples who lived and traded amongst us, but our beliefs were unique to us alone. We intermarried, we merged cultures and practices, but we never forgot the lessons of the Ice serpent. We were the guardians of the Rainbow Crystals, the gift from our ancestors, and the window to our world and the next. We safeguarded this portal, this thread through time, because humankind in its quest for power hadn't evolved to understand it. My father, his father, and the lineage that stretched the sands stood as protectors. I, being my father's only child and a woman, was in the precarious position of being the first female guardian, a factor that no one in the history of our tribe had given much thought to. It was assumed that I would marry young, to a man of my father's choosing, who would be "trained in the ways of the protector." But my father was slow to introduce me to any likely partner, and his sudden transition prevented an amicable arrangement. As a result, the whole palace was in a flux, with every handmaiden, worker, and soldier having an opinion one way or the other, and Fajah acting like the gatekeeper. I'd made my decision, I would marry Hasaan. In three days, he'd be my husband and King of Ku.

Hasaan, while respectful of the Rainbow Crystals, didn't obsess over the secrets. He didn't pummel me with questions, or beg me to unleash its power. He didn't adhere to ritual the way Fajah did, and he didn't find much use for seers either. He trusted that my knowledge was enough. "You're not the only one who can talk to the Universe," he said.

I knew our lore and rituals. I'd mastered the theory and philosophy. in that I could repeat it and converse amongst the religious leaders. I felt an inner sense of peace with our crystal meditations. But I felt there was more, much more. I suspected that none of my teachers had truly unlocked the crystals' secrets. We were dancing around it like my performances on the coast around the fire. I dreamed of sailing in an ark in the sky.

***

The Palace had been preparing for weeks. Anna oversaw the seamstresses and the making of my wedding wear. Four green crystals were embedded in the bosom of the blood-red gown, an Egyptian cotton dyed east of the ocean. Our greatest sword makers were bestowed the honor of crafting my crown, a silver bird's nest of dangling crystals, seashells, and gems, each reflecting the Crystal Cove. A fist-sized turquoise one in honor of our oracle glistened at the center. But as part of our culture's rules, I couldn't see any of these preparations. I made Anna describe everything to me in the strictest detail.

"Make sure I can stand up with the thing," I said to Anna as she described the crown's settings. "I don't want to fall from the weight of it. My duties will be heavy enough." Anna just wrinkled her nose, her dangling golden braid flitting with the breeze. Neighboring royalty were expected to attend, a sign of respect for my reign and that of my father's. But the affair would largely be a celebration for the people: feasts of lamb and fish, mango and breadfruit, dancing and music throughout the nights and the day. I love parties.

Yes, the wedding was in the final stages of preparation; but I felt uneasy, as if someone were keeping a secret from me. I noticed it first two weeks ago. Fajah likes to pace the courtyard in the moonlight when he's thinking. But lately, I've seen him on his knees, staring blankly into the sky as if he yearned for it to open up and swallow him. At first, I thought it was sheer nervousness and an annoyance at my defiant stance to marry Hasaan. The next night, I saw him do it again, this time with Anna at his side, both huddled on their knees ogling the stars.

"What are you doing?" I asked them. They glanced at one another and said something about praying for me and my happiness. But I didn't believe them. On the third night, I stepped into our Crystal Cove and heard whisperings, chants. I hid behind the cave's inner wall and peered over. Anna and Fajah were joined by Malik, the three chanting feverishly around the oracle. "What in the hell were they doing?" Something was desperately wrong. Were they conspiring against me? I couldn't be sure. These strange behaviors only validated my choice. I needed Hasaan to ward me against the weird ways of my own confidants.

I didn't have the gift of sight, but my confidants did. Every guardian in our line had eyes that could see the unseen. I was the first without it.

Yet, I was the protector of the Rainbow Crystals.

I feel alone in this palace. With my father gone, the whole town views me with suspicion. Can I build on the legacy of the ancestors? Am I an able successor to my father, The Great? Can I defend the nation in war? I could see doubt in Fajah's eyes. I saw pity in Anna's. She stopped giving me readings two moons ago. She said it would only upset the balance of my wedding day.

"You will do great things for your people," she said in our last session. "Look to the stars for your guiding light."

Malik was a strong arm for my father, a duty that stretched beyond his life. He was bigger than Chaga and Hasaan—a man whose might equalled his vigor for life. But Malik kept his thoughts to himself. With the exception of an occasional grunt or raised eyebrow, he knew his priority was to protect only. If I needed counsel, I had others to ask. But even he was a little more flippant than usual. Everyone else waited and watched. My struggles were their bedtime stories, their entertainment while washing, their small talk while walking the city streets.

Some nights I would go into the crystal chamber and meditate. Other nights, I'd read our scrolls. I read the heroic feats of my ancestors, of my father. A new parchment awaited my feats, too. For now, it was bare. But I felt no solace in these moments. In the past, I would sit with Chaga and we'd look to the night sky, fantasizing about a shooting star we could ride into the Milky Way. I felt peace in those moments. Today, my greatest solace came when I was with Hasaan.

Hasaan was still asleep in my chambers, so I went for a stroll in the garden. No sooner had I soaked in the morning dew, when Chaga snuck up beside me.

"Princess, we need to talk."

"There's nothing more to talk about, Chaga."

"This isn't about me, it's about you. I had another dream."

Chaga was riddled with dreams. And because our people had been rescued by the visions of the greats, anyone with the gift of deciphering dreams couldn't be dismissed—even if they were from a jealous lover.

"I keep dreaming about the Great Mountain. The two of us stand before it. Anna, Fayah, and Malik are by our sides. We look to the sky and suddenly vanish."

How puzzling, I thought.

"What does it mean?" I ask.

He took both of my hands and pulled me toward him. It felt as if he were going to kiss me.

"Our time here is over. You will be the last Guardian of the Great Crystal. Our people's rule here is done."

My heart grew heavy. A space between my brows tightened. I thought of Malik, Fajah, and Anna at the oracle. Was he serious?

"Do you see war?" I asked.

"No," he said.

"Do you see an asteroid?"

"No violence. We simply vanish."

"And where do we go?"

"To the source, the great beyond."

"When?" I asked. "When does this happen?"

"The time is near. Too close to say."

"And what about Hasaan?" I asked.

"I don't see him, Princess," he said.

"How convenient," I said.

The great oracle wrote that one day our people would become one with the source, our leaders would ascend, and the reign of human limitation would be no more. Father once joked that we'd all return to the SuperStar our people had come from. It was an allegory, we thought, but Chaga's dream said it was real.

"Fajah agrees."

"Always talking to Fajah before you talk to me. Whose protector are you, anyway?"

Chaga's eyes flashed with anger. I sighed.

"And how does this take place—this ascension?"

"We don't have much time. I just know that you, we, must fulfill the oracle."

"And my wedding?"

"It's not written."

I thought of the blank parchment with my name on it. I could feel the heat of coal burning my heart. He'd offended me. And the bite of the intent stung more than the reality itself.

"How come everything that I want is never written? How come these dreams about my future never come to me?"

"It's not your gift."

"And what is my gift?"

Chaga looked on, saying nothing.

"How do I know you're not making this up?"

"I don't need to. It will happen whether you agree to it or not."

In an instant, I hated him. I hated his honesty, I hated this destiny, but most of all I hated the oracle and the crystals.

"Don't you think it's odd that my destiny, as foretold by the oracle and the dreamers, never has anything to do with what I want? I am one of the most powerful women in this region, but I have no power over my own life? What's the point of power if you're a slave to fate?"

Sadness penetrated through his gaze. I was a different person to Chaga now. He looked upon me as if I were a stranger.

"You'd disavow the secrets of the crystals for him."

"That's ridiculous," I retorted.

A door opened and Hasaan emerged.

"Is there a problem?" Hasaan asked, sauntering our way. His shirt was removed, a wrap hugged around his legs.

"No problem. My people are ever watchful. Thank you, Chaga, for the news."

"What news? In two nights, I'll be the King of Ku. Surely I should know as well."

"And in two nights, you'll know," Chaga said and moved on.

"Another one of your former lovers, I assume," Hasaan said, a chuckle bellowing from his throat. But I didn't want to hear Hasaan's teasing. I needed to think, and I walked off through the garden. A small red bird soared, circled my waist, and flew off. I could hear the crunch of a fruit bite. Hasaan was watching me.

When I was out of his sight, I slipped into the cavern of crystals and stood before our beloved oracle. I fell to my knees waiting for my heart to glow. I needed reassurance. I needed an answer. I battered it with questions. I felt nothing. I heard nothing.

Chapter 8

Stormy Matters & Men with Xs

A rainstorm swept our small city. Although my room was a rainbow of silks and patterns, as the team of handmaidens busied themselves preparing for my wedding day, I longed to be in the clouds. The fuss of the wedding was a minor irritation. I had an ascension to consider. Anna noticed my pensive mood and ordered everyone out. They couldn't scurry away fast enough. And when the last of them shut the door, Anna turned to me.

"Talk to me, Princess."

"What could I tell you that you don't already know," I said. I walked to my window and looked to the clouds.

"I thought you were my friend, Anna."

"I am your friend."

"I'm sad, Anna. In my heart, I knew I would never be guardian of the crystals. I knew that no matter what I did, I would never be ruler of my father's land."

I loathed vulnerability. Emotion had so little room in the reign of a queen.

"I was very excited about the wedding," I said. "It's one of my greatest wishes."

"What's the other?" she said matter of factly.

"To destroy the oracle."

A water drop fell from the ceiling to the floor between us.

"It's a noose around our people's neck. We've latched ourselves to it, and I fear that in the wrong hands it could be misinterpreted. Like a dream," I said. "If it's destroyed, we'll have no worries."

"But the oracle isn't in the wrong hands."

I shoved my palms in hers.

"It will be if we leave," I said.

"Read them," I said. "Tell me you see me and Hasaan living in bliss."

She said nothing. I pulled my hands away and fell down in tears.

"We must go to the Mountain," she said. "Chaga will take us tonight."

"I will not," I said.

"But it is written," she said. "It will be the greatest moment for our people's history. Your story will be passed on for generations. Your sacrifice will bring new light to this world and the next."

Anna didn't seem like herself. My friend and protector was a stranger. Her cold eyes were the eyes of a mad woman. Fear was nestled in my belly. I gasped, afraid there would be no air in the room.

"Leave me," I said.

"But Princess."

I turned my head and she hurried off.

Remember the Time – Michael Jackson

The Midnight Fest is one of our cherished celebrations. Two nights before the royal wedding, both my family and Hasaan's are entertained by the best that both courts have to offer. Dancers with flaming sticks writhed before us. One man danced so fantastically, he spun like a storm and glided as if he walked on stardust across the moon. Just minutes before, a caravan of snake charmers and magicians weaved some spell on us; and before that, a hoard of dancing elephants graced the stage. Hasaan smiled my way, and I returned it with a nod. Anna and Fajah glided between the guests, charming as always, but they never took their eyes off me. I didn't see Chaga nor did I see Malik. On the day of the Midnight Fest, neither king nor queen was to speak to one another—a troublesome rule I would have to break.

I wasn't opposed to ascension, but I did take issue with the fact that this greatness I was to bestow I didn't feel deep within me. Why did Chaga feel it but not me? Why did Anna feel it but not me? This life-changing moment should fill me with joy. I should feel some sense of purpose, as if I'd known it all along. But I felt nothing. I did feel that I was the true Guardian of the Crystals, and I felt deeply that Hasaan was the love of my life. But this ascension thing simply did not ring true. Were Chaga and the others conspiring against me? After the Midnight Fest, I passed a note to one of the maidens who slipped it to Hasaan's men. He and I met at the Cliff of No Return. I shared my thoughts. He seemed perplexed.

"So you think the oracle isn't real?"

"Perhaps," I said.

"If the oracle isn't real and they're making it up, you won't ascend. You'll be here with me."

"And if it is?"

"Then you're the last Guardian of the Crystals."

"And what will you do?" I asked.

"Tell your story."

He kissed my forehead.

"You think this is funny," I said. "I don't think it's funny," he said, "preposterous, maybe, but not funny."

"My people and our beliefs aren't preposterous."

"I'm not talking about your people; I'm talking about you. What do you believe?"

"I don't understand what's being asked of me. I know that I want to be with you," I said.

"Why are you so concerned about me? Have you given any thought to this greater mission? As queen, your responsibility is to something higher first, your people second, me a distant third. Didn't Anna say this would change your world?"

"I won't be a slave to fate."

"Accept your mission, and you'll be chained to no one."

"No one is against us," he said, and he kissed my lips.

I longed to believe him and live in his trust.

"We'll get married on the mountain. If the oracle is true, when we wed, we'll all ascend and you will come with me."

"I should say goodbye to my mother," he joked.

"I'm serious."

He hugged me as the sun rose in the west. For the first time in a long time, I was happy.

"I wish that I could have this moment for 4 life." – Nicki Minaj

That night, I snuck out into the garden alone and gathered the herbs I would need. While I complained amongst the others, I didn't have the gift of sight. I knew my gift quite well. My gift was my affinity for alchemy and potions, a gift Father taught me and instructed me never to tell. If this ascension were real, Hasaan would be mine forever. Malik, Anna, and Fajah would simply have to deal with it. As I burned my mix into ashes, flicking both stardust and specks of Tiger Eye into the mesh, a glow came over me so strongly and suddenly, I felt the renewed strength of our ancestors and the ancient wisdom of our crystals. I found myself writing in the sand, my fingers moving through no effort of my own.

"I-C-E."

Snap. Through a slip of time, I was in a library with an infinite row of books. The rows stretched for miles and were as high as columns. I treaded lightly. A figure in green glided from one aisle to the next. I dipped behind a shelf. Don't reveal yourself, a voice so clearly said that I followed almost in fear. The figure, a petite woman with dark coils grabbed a book from the shelf, she flipped through it, but a black kitten purred and she stopped. The kitten slipped into another room, and she dropped the book on a short wood table before following the feline out the door. Counting the seconds, I tiptoed to the book. A photo of two women, one in a green dress, the other in a purple tunic, swords clashed, a blue crystal at the peak. I shut the book. The binding was etched in gold stitching—R.A.Y.L.A. Pages were obviously torn from the book, the back stuffed with

48

blank parchment. I flipped to a ripped page.

"You are the answer." – Ice

I heard a rustling. The kittens' purrs grew louder, closer. She was returning, this woman, whomever she was. I snatched the book and ducked behind another shelf. A hissing sound was by my ear, I turned to face a massive cobra. I disappeared.

The black sky engulfed me. The stars were whispering. I understood nothing. I understood everything. As quickly as it began, it ended. I was stretched out in the garden alone; Hasaan's turquoise stone in my right hand as I faced the sky, the thick blades of grass bedded at my back. A cat purred. I sat up and found the black cat atop the embossed book in my dream. Again, that name, R.A.Y.L.A.

There was more at work in my pending transformation—more than Chaga and the court knew, more than my people could ever grasp, more than I could ever want. I put the book in my bag of herbs. I would read it tonight.

The walk to my bedroom was longer than usual. Clarity made the hallways longer, I guess. The night was alive. I could feel the blades talking to the moon, just as I felt the wind dancing in the reeds.

The crystals were a symbol; a beautiful, valuable symbol, but a symbol nonetheless. While they held many treasures, both known and unknown, that would push the limits of science; the true gift of our people was embedded deep within me, deep within my father, deep within us all. The crystals were the reminder, a trick. The secret the warlords and competing rulers wished for was closer to them than their own nostrils. The "it's not written" clause, as the seal of my fate, was a joke. Who can write your own story but you? That was the secret shared with me by my father. My challenge, like that of my ancestors and all else who aspired to greatness, was to listen and allow the secret to be told through me. That is why this book was so odd. Someone was rewriting my story. Someone was trying to alter the pact made by souls before they entered the Earth plane. Someone, this woman in green, maybe? I did not know. The silence, the whispers in the garden, the chants, the dances were all tools to unleash the unknown within me. I read this book on this Rayla woman. Her story was not finished. The end was missing. Just like my end was missing. Someone was playing with time, snatching the future. I no longer questioned the ascension. I no longer cared about retaining my identity. I didn't question what was next. All that I needed to know would be revealed, and I was prepared for it. For now, I would keep Hasaan at my side; and this potion I created would ensure it. I poured a swallowful into my snake pendant. The rest, I would rub on his chest tonight.

Chapter 9

Juneteeth

THE streets were crowded with celebrants, each following our wedding parade to the Great Mountain. Four men carried me on my stilted caravan from the west, and Hasaan was riding a giant elephant with his caravan of soldiers from the east. We trekked through the town, past the grasslands, and across the burning sands to the Great Mountain. The sun was merciless, but our cheer was bountiful. The masses stayed at the Cliff of No Return and would watch our wedding in the shade. We royalty, and those enthused enough for the journey, were riding our beast of choice to the site. As usual, Fajah didn't like this idea one bit. It completely complicated the ascension. "We've become a traveling magician's act," he whined. I, on the other hand, found the whole thing to be rather exciting.

My little trick, my little secret.

This day would be my finest hour, and my people would remember this moment until the end of time. They needed that, I figured.

I smiled, nodding to the people as I sat several feet above them, hoisted in the air. Hasaan was several feet away, riding high as well. We looked to one another. His sparkling eyes and easy smile were the disposition of a confident man. He trusted me, he'd said. Whatever was to happen, would happen. As Guardian of the Crystal, I knew what was best. "I know," I'd told him.

Once at the Great Mountain, Malik and Chaga escorted me from my adorned wedding caravan. I nodded to both. They remained stone-faced and steady. I took several paces to Fajah, our festivities' priest. Hasaan joined my side. Fajah cleared his throat and began reading from the great scroll. His deep voice echoed across the canyon. The crowd cheered. As their cheering grew, Malik, Chaga, and Anna took their places. The three formed a triangle behind me, Fajah stepped directly before me, and the chants began. One rousing chorus, one clear cry to the universe. As their voices sped up, I felt the ground shift below me. I looked down, but there was no break in the ground. The vast canyon glowed. It no longer appeared real. Fajah took a step back. The world seemed to stretch, pulled like a reed in the wind. I felt light. The chorus grew louder, then silent. I heard a cry. The sky opened, pouring out a stretch of light. We—Fajah, I, Malik, Anna, and Chaga—were being pulled to the source. I looked below. My people were dotted along the coast, miles away. Hasaan stood speechless watching his bride ascend; a smile crept across his face. And just before we broached the horizon and I lost all consciousness, I soared like the red bird in my window and scooped up Hasaan. Anna gasped. Malik shouted. The crowd screamed. As quickly as the sky opened up, we'd vanished.

Chapter 10

Mermaid Marines

I popped out of the water, gasping for air. The warm ocean's waves swept me closer to the sea of sand. I could see figures to my far right on the beach. I climbed up the shore and looked about. The sun was beating my back. A forest due north, a stretch of sand five miles on east and west. A lone skyscraper eight to ten miles out to the east. Fifty yards west stood five individuals: one woman, four men; military maybe; one round, one crazy buff, two taller. The woman had a golden braid; no artillery; knives maybe. All wore fatigues. I looked down; I was in my underwear. Great. I walked toward them. They watched in silence.

I shook the water out of my head. The water wasn't salty. Fresh water, I assume. The taller of the bunch, a curly haired guy, chewing on tobacco, stepped forward.

"You Captain Blue?" I asked.

"Yes," he responded.

"You're under arrest for treason."

"Says who?"

A chopper lifted from the forest.

"It's time to go home."

The chopper landed, and the five walked single file on board. The other tall one glared my way. I traced my fingers along his hands, so slight that no one saw. I got aboard, and the craft lifted into the sky.

Chapter 11

Tin Man Tears

I'M being dragged through a sea of brisling cornstalks. I'm hoisted up and placed in the back of a truck. It goes black.

I awake. I'm on a table. Moulan is pressing both hands into my chest.

"Who are you?"

"Sergeant Bettye X."

"Who are you?"

"Sergeant Bettye...," my head was spinning. Where was I? Moulan's laser green eyes pierced my reality. "Rayla. I'm Rayla Illmatic

She breathes a sigh of relief. I sit up, and she hands me a cup of tea. The room is steely cold like a laboratory. The minty pomegranate liquid coats my throat. With each sip, the room transforms. The metal room is a parlor dipped in green velvets and silk. I'm lying on a red velvet couch. Moulan adorns a silk ruffled gown. I look about; Carcine and Delta Blue sit on opposite ends of a heavy oak table, arms folded, with smug looks on their faces.

"Can you explain this," she says shoving a fist-sized blue crystal in my face.

"It's turquoise, a blue crystal."

"I know what it is. But how did it get here?"

My head was spinning slower.

"How would I know?"

"Because it shouldn't be here. It belongs in the Crystal Cove."

"I need a debriefing."

Moulan threw up her hands in disgust.

"Now do you see," she screamed, glaring at Carcine. He nodded.

"It's like a gott damn hamster wheel."

"Be easy on her," Delta said.

Moulan grabbed a tea cup and handed it to me.

"Drink."

I obliged.

"Do you remember anything?" Moulan asked.

"Moulan, that's enough," Carcine said. He sat on the edge of the table, chest armor flanked over his light-blue tee shirt. He wore khakis and soiled boots.

"I thought you were dead," I said.

"This is what I'm talking about," Moulan shouted.

"How many times do we have to go through the same got damned routine?"

"It's your process," Carcine said calmly.

"I'm just working with what I have!" she screamed. She took a deep breath. "Let's begin again. My name is Moulan Shakur and ..."

"That's enough," Delta Blue chimed. "We've got time. It's all we do have. Get some rest, Princess." He walked out. Moulan followed. Carcine took my tiny hand in his and kissed it before leaving. He mouthed the words "thank you" before following the others out the door.

Four found, nine still missing. Mission not complete. We'd traveled the universe, and time, 97 times. At least I'd found Carcine. Moulan was frustrated,

55

but I felt complete.

She wants the secrets to the Crystal Cove. But I can't give them to her. None of us will. It's embedded deep within me, deep within her, deep within us all. We want to end the war, but we may have to save the universe. In the process, we'll save ourselves. Moulan, whom we thought was our greatest ally, is now the primary one standing between this world and the next. She's holding our planet hostage until she discovers the mysteries of time. Our futures are locked at her door. She, not Dirk, is our enemy. We can't let her stop our progress, snatch our futures because she's obsessed with the past. But we'll play her little game, finding The Missing, so we can overthrow her and her hold on our planet. One day, I will find my father. One day, we will get to modern-day earth. One day we'll reenter Shogun City. We might just have to use time travel to do it.

Besides, she doesn't have my book. She can't write my future.

It was still daylight; I exited Moulan's cottage door. Anna, Malik, and Fajah sat with the soldiers playing cards. Delta Blue, soaking in the red sunset, was rolling his tongue around that smelly smoking stick.

"She's on to you," Delta chipped, forming a cloud with his nostrils.

"What can she do about it? She's as locked in this time paradox as we are."

"Is she?" he asked.

"I found Carcine, didn't I?"

"That you did. You've got some skills. Some—" he said. I glared at him and returned my gaze to Carcine, who was sitting alone atop a grassy knoll overlooking the Field of the Yellow Lady.

"You might want to talk to him, though. He might not be as thrilled with this return as you are," Delta added.

"Oh, really?"

"Just telling you like it is. It's awfully comfy being King," he said, flashing a grin as he waved at the red-headed soldier by the camp. "Everyone's not up for the fight."

"You don't know everything, Delta Blue."

"And neither do you, Princess. But I don't try to," he said, walking off to join the smiling redhead. He turned around.

"Besides, I've got all the time in the world," he said, stealing a grin before strolling back to attend to his lady in waiting.

Jealous lovers live forever.

I joined Carcine, snuggling beside him. He kissed my neck, and we watched the sun descend into the evergreen forest. A cool breeze whipped by, and I shivered; I looked over my shoulder. Moulan was peering through her cottage window, watching us.

I am ready for her challenge. I know who I am.

"Rayla," Carcine said. I'd almost lost myself in my flint of aggression. He kissed my forehead.

"I love you," he said, as if I didn't know. "You mean the world, this world to me. But this is not our time." My smile cracked. He cupped my head in his and placed it on my heart. "I'll always be here," he said. With that, he rose to his feet and vanished.

I screamed. The few remaining soldiers in the camp raced my way, but their heartfelt attempts at comfort did nothing. Anna threw her arms around me. Malik tried to hold the others back. Fajah fell to his knees in prayer. Delta wouldn't look at me. I couldn't stop screaming, and yet I heard no sound. The thunder was caught in my throat.

Chapter 12

What Time Is It?

"I don't know if I can make myself any clearer about the nature of this assignment, Bettye. Love, in this space, is not an option. Is that understood?"

I nodded.

"Can you remember anything else about the Crystal Cove? Anything I don't know, significant? Any names, any inscriptions, messages?"

"I was blindfolded most of the time. Heard some chanting. I don't know Vietnamese. Couldn't make it out."

"Chanting ... like a song?"

"Drumming mostly. Can you tell me what you're looking for? That would help."

"How can I know what I'm looking for if I haven't found it?"

"Understood."

"I studied that crystal of yours; not much to it. It must not work in this world."

"I guess not."

"A religious symbol maybe."

"Probably."

"That'll be all. You can go back to your barracks. Oh, and keep it."

"What?"

"The crystal, keep it; a reminder of your travels; something to pass on to the kids."

"Oh, right."

"Not every prisoner of war lives to tell about it."

"Right."

"Spy work is spy work. Better than being an informant. Blue, will you take the lady down to the press corps first. A reporter, a Carcine Blackfoot is waiting for you."

"Why?"

"Says he wants to tell your story. Feels obligated, the two of ya being from the same hometown and all. Says he remembers you, something about integrating a Woolworths. You do some Freedom Riding before the war? Well, a hero's a hero. You, Ms. X, are a war hero. Hope you don't mind us blowing your cover."

"Not at all."

"The media's gonna have a field day, and we need the good press. Gotta mark our progress. Got it?"

"Got it."

"Good. Oh, and don't mention Sergeant F. He's keeping a low profile on this one. Doesn't want to bring any attention to the Mrs. and all."

"The Mrs.?"

I guess he didn't get around to yapping about her. It happens. Uh, Blue, please take care of the lady. And again, welcome back to the United States. Washington, D.C welcomes you. It's a lot of opportunity for a woman like yourself; 1971's a helluva year.

"Click your heels three times if you believe."— Lena Horne, Glinda the Good Witch

Do you still use the word time, I wonder? I digress. You're here for the story, my never-ending story, which, for sanity's sake, I've whittled down to one thought and one person at a time. Two hearts and one arrow. My beginning is my end. So I'll begin by moving backwards. We'll moonwalk—literally. How shall I begin? Ah, yes. It all began with a white light. It all ended with a white light—a brilliant white light that cut the blue black sky in two.

Once upon a time

The Book of Rayla

Rayla Redfeather

&

The Return of Bettye x

2

Chapter 13

The Tree of Life

ICE had ripped the sky open and was pelting me with warm water. The rain drops were the size of snowballs; but the water was so warm, I found no need to stop my carnage. So I swung the ax again.

T.I.M.B.E.R.

Another tree crashed to the ground and there was no sound. Simply amazing. I couldn't get past the inversion of natural law in Moulan World. Just like I couldn't get past Carcine's haunting words before he vanished. This is not our time.

"Sitting on the dock of the bay, wasting time." – Otis Redding

Bastard. I brushed my hand over my face to clear my vision, only to have another water ball smash me in the face. My stance was weakening in the muddy sinkholes. I bent my knees to balance my stance and was hurled in the thigh with three more whopping water balls. I fell to my knees. The arrogance of him knowing something that I didn't and his deadpanned contentment to keep it to himself. I'd circled the galaxy and back, only to have my heart broken by the one who inspired the journey in the first place.

"Then why'd you ask me to find you, if you were content in some self-prescribed exile?" I screamed, lunging onto a hollow boulder to regain my stance. I knew he heard me, wherever he was. Sound might not reverberate in this Moulan world, but I knew he felt me. The sting of my pain had ripped through time. Too bad I couldn't feel his response. Another water ball smacked me in the face. This was starting to feel personal.

63

"No cloud in my storms. I let it rain, I hydroplane into fame."

– Rihanna, Umbrella, Earth, 2007

That is, if he had responded. I would like to think that he would. Maybe one day I'd evolve to hear it. While I tried to convince myself that anger was the more resolute defense to shield my wounded heart, I believed that there was more—more to his words, more to this mission. Or maybe I found solace in some fantasy belief that Carcine cared, that he harbored a secret that time would unfold. Carcine, I reminded myself, is not all-knowing, and neither was I.

He knew something, though. He had a mission of his own. I had mine, and beyond this war, our paths were aligned in a larger cause I knew little about. I was convinced that Moulan had our world locked in time. I will confront her about it. That is when I figure out the question. I needed to think, so I chopped wood. I swung the heavy ax so hard, I was mildly surprised that it didn't bend with one blow. But I found the swinging motion comforting. I liked the gleam of the ax in the moonlight. I liked the heaviness in the swing. I loved the cracking sound of the ax to the tree. And when the tree fell, I reveled in the silence.

"Now what?" I yelled, waiting for Ice to respond.

Thunder crackled softly. Lightening flashed just quickly enough to silhouette the monster tree before me. Twenty meters thick, its skyscraper branches twisted about like spider webs and scorched the sky. No point in putting an ax to this one. I fell to the ground instead and cozied up along a soft patch of soil at the base of the trunk. It was the one area of the forest free of rainfall.

"Psssst," a voice whispered.

I looked up to the web of branches and a golden rope fell, the tassel dangling before my face.

"Whose there?" I whispered.

No answer. I tugged on the rope. It felt pretty secure. My new adventure begins. I grabbed the rope and prepped to scale the massive trunk. But before I could get my footing, I was flung into the air. Good thing I held on tightly.

THE TREE OF LIFE

I landed on a fat branch. I walked the branch like a plank all the way to the golden door emblazoned in the tree trunk. With each wobbly step, the door cracked open just wide enough for me to walk inside. Then it shut.

Chapter 14

Maggot Brains

THE room was bright light white, and it took a moment for my eyes to adjust just enough to decipher the floor from the wall. Everything in this room was white: white floors, white walls, and white splotches of paint on white mats in thick white frames. A white couch in white fur lay square before me, with a stack of white book covers with white pages. I wondered if the ink was white, too.

"Boo," a deep voice howled. I whipped around only to see Delta Blue and his candid smirk. Wearing his blue-stained warrior ware and pitch-black glasses, I was, despite myself, happy to see him. "You expecting a white rabbit?"

"What is this?" I asked.

"About time you started asking some questions. Solving the mysteries of life on your own. Tsk, tsk, tsk," he said shaking his head. He plopped down into the fuzzy couch and kicked his legs up. The steel toe of his boot gleamed like the devilish twinkle in his eye.

"Have a seat," he said. I thought he wanted me to join him on his lap, but he pointed to a shiny white couch behind me.

"I'm muddy," I said.

"And?" he responded

I sat down, slipping a bit on the surface. The mud meshed into the whiteness, but the whiteness remained.

"I call it my lair," he said. The place was as big as it was small. The whiteness of it all blurred the dimensions. The ceiling could very well be the floor. The four walls might as well be the white space between us. "You really don't remember me?" he asked.

"If you're talking about that escapade in East Africa, the answer is yes."

"I'm not talking about that. I'm talking about us, here on Planet Hope. "

"That was nothing," I quipped, referring to our tryst beyond Moulan's cottage.

"I'm not talking about that either."

"What should I remember, Delta?"

Like a sorcerer, he flipped his left wrist and two palm-sized crystal balls emerged. He circled the sparkling stones in his palm, and with ease they morphed into a red feather.

"You a magician now?"

"That and so much more."

"So this is a vortex, a protected zone," I said.

"Uh huh. Keep going."

"In this space there is not time."

"Uh huh," he said.

"Beyond these walls, time has been locked in some crazy time continuum."

"Uh huh."

"And Moulan has us trapped."

"You can leave whenever you want," he added, sliding one finger up the spine of the feather.

"But there's nowhere to go. Just perpetual war. Or—"

"You can unlock the secret to the Crystal Cove."

"Or kill Moulan."

"Now, I can't let you do that."

"She's stolen our future," I said.

"She's safeguarding it. Just a little task she has to oversee until we find the Missing. It was the only way she could stop the Dirk; the only way to stop the transmitters he was emitting in the air to read thought patterns. The only way to neutralize the thought surveillance. His power can't get any greater."

"Nor can we end the war."

"We can end the war after we find the Missing, or after you stop looking for a certain someone who is not among the Missing."

"Then where is he?"

"If I remember correctly, he said it's not your time."

In a flash, I popped up, drawing my sword. He matched my timing and drew his.

"This is pointless, Rayla. You're fighting the wrong battle."

I went for his heart. He blocked so fiercely that I flew back, my back slamming into the wall.

"I didn't become a legend for nothing. And what happened to your sword work? It used to be better than this. They really did get to you, didn't they?" he said.

The tree shook. At first, I thought I was dizzy. I tried to shake it off, but Delta's eyes narrowed and I knew something was wrong. The tree shook again. We knew this treacherous quake well. Tigers were one on the prowl.

"I thought this area was protected," I said.

Delta grabbed my hand and pulled me up in one sweep. He tucked his sword away, clutched the red feather in the other hand, and we ran through the white wall into the inner sanctuary of the tree. We slid down a massive pole into a dark cavernous maze I'd never seen before. The maze was lined with ivy-laced bricks. We splashed through the thick layer of water lining the floor. We ran like the wind, but the maze felt safe, almost familiar. Delta pulled me along. We ran smack into a brick wall, and a trap door shut behind us. He rapped on the wall three times and it vanished. We were in an ancient kitchen. Steel so shiny you could see your own reflection lined the countertops. A young woman in a pale pink dress and apron tied at her waist was stirring. Her back was to us. Her bluntly chopped hair dusted her shoulders, and her small waist was accented with a large bow in the small of her back. She was in no hurry to greet us, but eventually she dusted off her hands and turned around. Her hair and dress swirled a bit as she spun. She removed the apron, tossed it on the counter and put on a pair of long white gloves that matched the string of balls on her neck. Her large dark brown eyes were engaging. She wore a matter-of-fact friendliness about her.

"Good day, Delta."

"Good day," he responded, sounding more like a boy than the warrior I knew.

"Good day to you, Rayla."

"Good day," I said.

Delta took a seat at the kitchen table and motioned for me to follow. The woman looked at us briefly, crossed the room, and pulled out a bottle of wine. She popped the cork, poured three glasses, and sat them before us. , She held her glass in the air. Delta and I followed.

"To the rebellion," she said.

"The rebellion," we echoed.

She guzzled the drink down in one swipe, her long neck arched so far back, and even Delta frowned.

Chapter 15

When a Chair's Not a Chair

I remembered this woman. She was Rita, the lady Sui Lee and I visited when I was 12. Sui Lee and I were draped in invisible black clothes and slipped in through a backdoor into a kitchen that looked much like this one. I remember her pearls. I remember her oddly suited apron. I remember the shiny dagger she kept in her apron pocket. I remember shortly after meeting her, the women who raised me in the Enchanted Forests had me put to sleep. Sui Lee said it was the only way to keep the Dirk from penetrating my mind. I woke up when I was 21. I was paired with Carcine's task force. I became the rebel strategist and learned the terrain to isolate and destroy the Dirk for good. Sui Lee advised me until she was captured by the Tigers.

"Whew," Rita said, shaking her head and tossing her hair. She sat down beside us, throwing her hands up slowly to stretch. She yawned, her mouth stretching wide enough to see her tonsils. She eventually covered her mouth and followed it up with a cracking of the neck.

"You're Rita," I said. She smiled sweetly, the sugar popping from her temples.

"I was very, very close to your guardian Sui Lee. I admired her. I admired your father. He was quite the man," she said, a dazed look in her eye. "They are valiant heroes. They will not be forgotten. "She poured another glass of her red elixir. Delta Blue and I hadn't finished ours, and she didn't replenish it.

"We've made some progress since the day I saw you last. We halted the mind surveillance. We prevented Dirk and the Tigers from penetrating Shogun City. We've kept the mazes relatively clear. And Moulan, for now, is protected. All else is perpetual motion this way. The war continues, but there is an end in sight. I hear you brought back a crystal from the Crystal Cove."

"I did," I said, not sure how Rita was aware.

"Anything else?" she asked.

Rita's brown eyes were sparking with question marks, but for some reason I didn't trust her. Reflecting on my sleeping years always made me feel uncomfortable. And there was something about Rita that made those lost years feel close at hand, as if I could slip away at any moment. Why, I wondered, had Delta brought me here? I decided to respond to her question, although I knew my answer wouldn't be satisfactory. "Three astronauts," I responded.

She smiled.

"Is it true that she has a book with everyone's name in that library of hers?"

"Hard to say. It's quite massive," I said. Rita leaned forward.

"How did you manage to get yours?"

"Rita," Delta interjected. "She doesn't know."

Rita leaned back. She kicked her leg on the table, her pink shoes rested on thin metal stilts and she was dangling on the table's edge. She pulled a cigar from under her skirt. Delta offered her a light and she smoked.

"Not so very long ago, when Moulan banged up our astronaut operation, I led the effort to keep her in hiding just long enough for her to figure out his vortex protection. When I ordered her to halt the war, I didn't expect her to steal the damned future and rule over the book of our life." Rita took another drag. "I'm two months pregnant," she said. "I've been two months pregnant for the last 75 years. Why? Because Moulan can't figure out how to unwrinkle this time paradox. Do you know what it's like to have morning sickness for 75 years?"

Rita was crazed. We had not been fighting for 75 years.

She kicked her legs up and folded them neatly under the table. She grabbed her stomach, arched her back, and fled to a pail in the corner and vomited. She grabbed a pink napkin, wiped her mouth, and returned to her seat looking exhausted. She took a breath, composed herself, grabbed her smoking stick, and took a puff.

"You and Moulan are the only ones with your own books. The only ones who can write your story, in this world at least," she said, her smoke circling into tiny ringlets that dissipated as they reached the ceiling. "Do you remember what happened after you visited me with Sui Lee?" she asked. The smoking stick was intoxicating, and I felt myself growing light-headed.

I could feel the hairs on the back of my neck stiffen, uneasiness tickling up my spine.

"I had no life until I was 21," I said.

Rita giggled. Then her giggle ballooned into a hearty chuckle. The laughs came so fast that she doubled over and nearly choked. I looked to Delta who was fixated on the swirling smoke. Rita fanned herself, cleared her throat, and resumed.

"Hey, Delta, ya hear that. Mami said she had no life?" Delta wouldn't look her way. She turned her gaze towards me.

"No, you had quite the life—a life to envy, a life to die for," she said. "We took great pains to make sure you didn't remember. But that time is over. Now you have to know," she said. "Our world is depending on it."

Delta was twiddling the red feather between his slim fingers. Rita snatched it.

"Does this look familiar?" she asked, clutching the feather like a blade that she waved like a reed in the wind.

"Sui Lee called me Redfeather. It was a code name," I said.

"Hey, Delta, should I tell her the story or should you?" Rita asked, narrowing her dark eyes. I glared at Delta. Delta avoided me but took my hand in his. I pulled it away. Rita giggled.

"Should I tell the story or should you?" she hissed.

"Your stories are filled with such charm, I'd just pale in comparison," said Delta sheepishly.

Rita looked from Delta to me.

"Suit yourself," she said.

Chapter 16

Red Queens Love Ice Cream, Too

ACCORDING to Rita, she, along with Sui Lee and the Sisterhood of the Enchanted Forest, believed my life was in grave danger. The Dirk was on a warpath looking for me. In fact, second to Moulan, he wanted the minds and hearts of all the children of the Missing. Being the daughter of Illmatic made me a special target, and the bounty on my head topped them all. The Ladies of the Enchanted Forest had protected me as long as they could; but Dirk's mind-wave project was diminishing their force fields, and Sui Lee believed it was just a matter of time before my mind was under siege. That's when she risked her life to find Rita. Rita was married to Cheyenne, second in command to the Dirk, and leader of the Tigers. Before the war, Rita and Sui Lee were best friends. Rita's mother was one of the architects of Shogun City. Although the city had decided to halt the entry of newcomers, largely to protect themselves from the Dirk, Rita felt she could slip me in. And she did. The Shogun City elite were suspicious of my arrival. Rita was too close to the Dirk; and they feared that if in a bind, she would give access to Dirk and Cheyenne. They were also suspicious of me. I was daughter of Illmatic, a fact they revered as much as they feared. Illmatic was never one to play by the rules. I was also blood granddaughter of Ice, the planet's first griot. While I had royal blood or was legacy by Shogun City standards, I was not likely to conform to their status-based culture.

"They feared that once you were of age, you would take over the city," Rita said.

Shogun City was founded by the first wave of the earth's wealthy ones who came to the planet on space tourism missions. Planet Hope's original inhabitants, a team of scientists, futurists, and metaphysicians weren't too keen on space tourism, preferring to cultivate a true society first. Nevertheless, the trips helped to fund their exciting new endeavor, so they went along with it. Team Planet Hope, as the newcomers called themselves, among other things were also dedicated to building a society with no class system. Earth's elite had no issue with this until earth ended space tourism and began the planet lottery, and a heap of people from all walks of life were siphoned to the planet. Then came the undesirables. While Team Planet Hope were thrilled by the exciting new dynamics, the space tourists with their permanent vacation homes were not. At least, some of them weren't. And those few went off to create their own city to preserve Planet Hope's values as they saw fit. They named themselves the Originals and called their town Shogun City. But when Earth began to dump its undesirables in masses on Planet Hope and insisted on draining the planet of its crystals and natural resources, actions that would destroy the society-building efforts, Team Planet Hope waged the battle for independence.

With Team Planet Hope juggling so much and eventually leading the path for independence, they allowed Shogun City's Originals to form a society of their own. The Originals played a big role in Planet Hope's independence. Many of them were also Master Architects, and they created temples and facilities that rivaled those in Obama City. They even cloned themselves to build the city quickly and dismantled the clones in accordance with Planet Hope's ban of the practice. However, after independence, Team Planet Hope went to investigate Shogun City a little deeper. Going beyond the crystal palaces and entertainment forums, they weren't pleased with their discoveries. For one, Shogun City had created its own military, a secret elite fighting team aptly dubbed the Shangos. Planet Hope forbid the creation of a military. Secondly, Shogun City's Originals weren't incredibly hospitable to newcomers, who after a few days in the city often felt as if they didn't belong and moved elsewhere. They had a unique style of dress reminiscent of the traditional royalty of Earth's old world: dresses fit for Katherine the Great, ornate royal Kimonos, Egyptian crowns, royal kente cloth. Pick a period of Earth's old world styles of the royals and the Originals dawned it. They also used archaic feudal terms. Calling one another prince or princess, queen or king, sun and earth, knight and more.

Most disturbing, Team Planet Hope discovered that the Originals had created an extensive underground maze system that connected the underworld. All of this took place without the Team Planet Hope oversight. The Originals convinced the team that this was all for protection. That they would never use the Shangos to undermine the planet, nor would they take advantage of their underground maze, which literally connected them to every city and portal on the planet. In fact, the Originals taught the team the path of the maze. But some on Team Planet Hope were convinced that the Originals were hiding something. Oddly, the intuits on the team couldn't quite figure it out.

So shortly after Sui Lee and I met Rita, I was told I'd be put to sleep. Instead, I was unconscious just long enough to get me into Shogun City where

I was placed with Edna and Jaggi Delight, a fanciful couple with a penchant for the eccentric. Sui Lee didn't want me to get lost in their royal snobbery, though; and she insisted that in addition to living with the Delights, that I be trained by the Shangos.

"Shango. Does that word feel familiar to you?" she asked, her eyes like lasers penetrating my skull.

"You took great lengths so that it wouldn't," I responded. Rita raised an eyebrow and continued.

"You were among their best students, second to Delta Blue," she said. "But you had a special gift that the others didn't; or at least, that's what your teachers said. But they kept your special talent very, shall I say, mum. They were quite hush hush about it."

"Such a pity that you don't know what it is," Rita chirped. "But you'll need to know what it is, if we're to move forward. And I would tell you, but I don't have the foggiest idea."

What little affection I had for Rita and her camaraderie with Sui Lee had vanished. This meeting was a bit cavalier for my taste, and I detested that they knew more about me than I knew about myself. It would be comforting to dismiss it all as make believe. But her words were prickly truths. I was vulnerable. I was exposed. I swallowed my emotions into my stomach. I believed her because she had no reason to lie. I believed her because deep down I knew there was more to my life, too. I had always been haunted by a sense of destiny that felt beyond my reach. Now I realize it was a history yet to be revealed. But Rita had no answers for me. I seemed to be the answer to her question. Rita is a woman with a wish, and I was brought here to grant it. My self-discovery was just a means to her end. I sent 'if-looks-could-kill glances to the uncharacteristically quiet Delta who refused to look my way. Instead, he kept his eyes on the red feather between the three of us.

"So, I'm going to need you to do something for me," said Rita, cracking an easy smile. "I want my book. You get my book; I'll get you back into Shogun City."

"And why would I go back to Shogun City? "I asked.

"Because you don't know who you are. And that gift you have will save us all."

"But why do I need you to get back to Shogun City?"

Rita smiled. "Because I have the key," she said. "And lover boy Delta has some skeletons of his own that don't make his return so easy either," she

74

quipped.

At that moment a key jostled and a door unlocked. Rita's face was flush with horror. Delta Blue took my hand, and we stepped quietly to a cobblestone wall. He wrapped three times, and in a flash we were back in the maze. But instead of running through like we did before, Delta waited, his ear to the wall. I felt them, too.

TIGERS.

I rapped on the door three times; Delta was behind me. We were back in the kitchen, just in time to catch Rita stabbing one Tiger with her dove-tailed knife, ripping it from his chest and stabbing another coming from behind her. I pulled my sword, cutting off the head of one and slashing the arm of another. Delta leaped forward and swung low, stopping two more from pelting through the door. He pinned the door shut, I grabbed Rita, and the three of us went through the cobblestone wall. The muddied water on the maze floor was rising.

"They're trying to penetrate the maze," Delta said.

"Follow me," said Rita.

We ran behind her, diving left and right as we scaled the winding tentacles. There were so many forks and dips in the sparsely lit tunnels; it was shocking that anyone could remember the way. But I felt alive in these walls. My skin prickled with an instinct that only underscored Rita's story, a story that in our short conversation, I was still mulling over to determine its truth. Just as I tried to zone out and reflect, we hit a dead end. Footsteps were behind us. Fifty or so Tigers were on our trail.

Rita was patting the wall with her hand.

"Come on, where are you?" she whispered.

"Looking for this," Cheyenne said, emerging from a shadow. An attractive man with wide shoulders and a glow-in-the-dark smile, his dark eyes shot through us like lightning bolts. He dangled a silver key in his hand; a dark body suit clung to his body like a second skin and his anger made the cobblestone walls turn blood red with heat. "My Rita," he continued. His heavy voice made my stomach drop. Shaking his head in painful disappointment, he looked at his wife with the anger of a man whose heart had been stabbed. "All these years we've been trying to defeat Shogun City, find it, learn the maze, find the maze, and my lovely wife was sitting with the key all along." He looked to us. A hint of shock flashed through his eyes. "Is this Delta Blue?"

Delta reached for his sword, but was thrown back into the sizzling wall. Cheyenne was using brain waves to pin him. Delta was immobilized. I attempted to reach for my sword, but my arms wouldn't move. Was I afraid? Had fear left me motionless? I felt trapped in my own body, thankful, that for the moment I could at least breathe.

"Don't," Rita screamed.

"And who is this?" he said, looking me over. The Tigers had encroached. We were cornered. Although I couldn't move, straining to do so made no sense, I relaxed. I focused on my breath.

"I can't read you," he said. "How odd." He held up a scanner, waving it along my face down to my torso. He flagged it by my heart and stared. His eyes were coal black, no retina, all pupils. He bore the eyes of an animal, not a man; and something about this realization made me forget about my inability to move and just look. Who has black eyes? "No facial recognition, no heart reading, no brainwaves," Cheyenne bellowed. "Tigers, I think we've found a ghost." The men laughed.

"Cheyenne," Rita pleaded. "Let's end this now. The war doesn't have to continue."

"And for you it won't," he said.

Rita screamed, but it was too late. Cheyenne inflicted a brain wave, and she collapsed to the floor.

I stood motionless, mesmerized by these strange black eyes.

"She's protecting you," Cheyenne said. "The question is why?" He eyed the silver key, rotating it in his slender fingers as if he were looking for a secret to unfold. But I wanted to know what lay behind the black eyes. I looked as deeply into the abyss as I could and felt the chain on my brain crackle. I was free.

A battle cry bellowed from the Tigers in the back. Before the first one could pounce, I reached for my darts in my hip pocket and hit him in the neck. The key flew into my hand and Cheyenne dropped to the floor. The Tigers stormed me. They came so fast and so hard, my slashes were a total blur. But one by one they fell to the ground and vanished. I was horrified. These hulking undefeatable figures vanished like ghosts in the wind. I turned to Delta Blue, who was still pinned to the wall. I pierced Cheyenne's powerful brain wave and Delta was free. I crouched next to Rita and placed my hands on her hip, I allowed light to fill my fingertips, and she coughed as she pushed back to the wall. Cheyenne lay coiled on the ground; he was all that remained of what should have been carnage. But Cheyenne was the sole body.

"He's immobilized, "I said. "He'll come too, eventually."

"We can hold him hostage," Delta said.

Rita cleared her cough and crawled to Cheyenne. "That's not my husband," she said. "Cheyenne passed away years ago." She placed her right hand on his forehead. "He's a double created by the Dirk." With that, Rita cracked his neck. "I've been living in terror. I'm so glad that you're here."

Delta and I looked to one another. The Dirk has a fleet of flesh and bone doubles? How many are there? Who are they? What about the Tigers, and why did they vanish like images projected from afar?

"We have to seal off this half of the maze. We can't have the Dirk learning the underworld," I said.

"No worries. This is the outer crust. We haven't gotten to the real maze yet," said Delta.

Rita stood and brushed strands from her jet-black hair back under her pointy ears. She stuck out her palm. "Key please," she said. Her clarity was startling. I handed it to her. "As I said, I need that book. Don't stand in my way when I come to get it." Rita turned her back and walked towards the shadows.

"You can't go home, Rita. They'll find you," I said, realizing the irony.

"Who exactly is 'they'?"

She stopped and turned to face us.

"I'm going to a place where I should have gone long ago," she said.

"Why didn't you go home before?" I shouted, surprised by my own fervor. It was an imposing question, but this inability to break free made no sense. Rita had the key to unlock her own prison, and yet she remained until my arrival? "Like I said, Sui Lee was a friend of mine. Get my book, Missy, and we'll talk this debt owed over a red one. " She turned and strode into the shadows. I listened until the click of her knife-long stilettos were muffled and elapsed into silence.

Chapter 17

Blade Lives

WE were at a fork in the road. Rita walked north. I looked west and east, and marched eastward. Delta Blue was on my heels. "You're going the wrong way," he quipped.

"How do you figure?" I responded. Delta Blue, for all his talents, wasn't much of a mind reader. If he thought I was going to Shogun City, he was mistaken. "So we knew one another," I said. "Was that your big secret? I could have guessed that," I said.

"Rayla," he said, trotting to catch up with me. I stopped and turned to face him or rather the muddy stench on the floor. Delta tipped my head up with his fingertips and made me look in his eyes. He was so beautiful that my seesawing emotions ebbed a bit, but I wouldn't turn away or he wouldn't let me escape his loving gaze until I'd calmed down. A litany of water ball moments pelting you from the sky was not what life was supposed to be. I longed for a comfort that I had no recollection of. Brief moments like this had become my anchor in the storm. The thought of these lost, invisible years made me want to cry; but I refused, and Delta's love wasn't going to make me. "Look around you," he said. I looked at the loosely plastered bricks and the coiled ivy that twisted in knots like a snail. The plant, which I'd spotted earlier, was a tender reminder of the sweetness of life.

"This was our place," he said, stepping back as if to give me the space to remember. Calmness laced Delta's aura. I'd never known him to be calm, ever.

I looked around again wanting to feel the memory, some sliver of what must have been a beautiful moment in my lost life; but the rush of questions pelted me. My uncertainty floated to the surface of my mind, and the glint of magic faded. All I saw were old crackling bricks, ivy, and mildew. I placed my hands on the bricks. The warmth was comforting, familiar even, but I recalled nothing. Delta's eyes had such longing in them; I wanted to remember whatever it was he was talking about. But too much was happening for me to give the moment its due. I felt a desire to connect but nothing else. And even that desire was second to the mission. We had a planet to save and astronauts to find. I shook it all off—the doubt, the love, the anguish—and took control of my thoughts.

"Will this road take me to Moulan's?" I asked.

"Yes," he said, as if he'd been defeated. I ignored his feelings and off we headed, back to Moulan's.

***

The door slammed behind us, and we were back in Delta's Lair. I found a white teakettle with a white liquid and poured it into two thimbles of a cup. One for me and one for Delta. I handed one to Delta and he reluctantly obliged.

"To the Lost Years," I said, holding my thimble in the air. Delta didn't respond. He didn't like the joke.

Delta was drunk with silence. He didn't take a sip.

"Those Tigers disappeared under my blade," I said.

"I know."

"They aren't real," I said.

"They sure do fight like they're real."

"If they aren't real, that gives us an upper hand. We can win the war." Are they digital projections, I wondered. The Dirk is projecting digital images? But Delta, it seemed, was elsewhere, reminiscing on a time he knew I didn't remember, as if trouncing down the Lost Years would end the war. My blood was still racing from my fight with ghosts and I didn't have the patience for his sentiments.

"Do you really think that more wallowing in our own past will restore this planet? It's not about me, or us. It's about the people and freedom on Planet Hope."

79

"You don't want to know," he said.

"And you're afraid to tell me," I reminded him. "And I won't be cornered into doing anything by someone whose dangling information before my eyes like it's a golden carrot. Three down, nine more to go."

"Alright, Princess. You know what's best."

"Why are you so condescending?" I asked. I was the one with the missing past, a fact for which he had zero empathy.

"Unfortunately, your allegiance is to the virtues of the Sisterhood," he said. "Shogun City was your home, too."

I had no idea what Delta was talking about and at the moment didn't care. I refused to feel guilty about a past he was complicit in hiding from me.

"Maybe you should take a nap and remember it all in a dream," he said snidely, before exiting through a rectangle in the wall and shutting it behind him. The white teakettle shook with the weight of the door. But he must have regretted his silliness. As quickly as he left, he returned.

"I apologize," he said, with an awkward sense of duty, as if his earlier pouting was just a stitch of unprofessionalism and not the emotional need that surfaced.

"Forgiven," I said. He nestled on his fuzzy white couch, turned his back, and dozed off.

I needed to rest before I confronted Moulan. While I wanted to resist Delta for the sake of resisting, I was exhausted. I removed my boots and curled up on a couch opposite his.

I closed my eyes, but I couldn't sleep. Delta was right. I was afraid to learn more about Shogun City. I was fearful of the fact that I could live a life that I didn't remember, and I now felt closeted by the cloud of mystery. Who else knew about my missing past? Did my team know? Did Carcine know? What happened? Who was I, and what kind of life did I have with Delta Blue. We were lovers? Was that the big secret? What did it mean? And what was this gift Rita mentioned?

I always had abilities, fighting instincts that were second nature to me. When Carcine trained me, the strategies he taught I already knew. He was always bewildered by my knack for soaking up strategy, intelligence. There is no privilege in war. Skill and talent is king in small battalions aiming to overthrow a dictator. Although some suspected I rose so quickly because of Sui Lee's guidance or Carcine's interest in me, it became obvious to all of them that I was simply among the best.

Eventually I fell asleep. I dreamed of my past life as a princess sitting in the Crystal Cove. I dreamed of Hassan whispering in my ear before our wedding night. As he kissed me, I was aware it was just a dream and awoke to see Delta sunk in his white couch, studying my feather.

"When Cheyenne threw me against the wall, he penetrated my force field," he said. "He couldn't penetrate yours."

"He didn't get a reading either," I said, strapping up my boots.

"Why do you think that was?" he asked.

"I'm not in the system," I said. "I'm not in the global database." Sui Lee took great strides to ensure that I was untraceable after the Original Illmatic was captured. Once we went to the Enchanted Forest, no one, outside of the rebels, ever saw me again. Well, at least that's what I thought before I learned about this stint in Shogun City. I really didn't feel like thinking about any of it.

"Neither am I," he said.

"You sure about that?" I responded. "You sure some of those friends of yours in Shogun City didn't have you plugged in?"

"Positive," he said, still studying the feather in his hand.

"If you're trying to say I'm a double, let me be the first to say that you are letting your imagination go wild," I responded.

"You're not a double ... I don't think," he said flashing a grin.

I ignored him.

"But you might have one," he added.

"Well wouldn't that be grand," I said. The thought of it made my stomach turn.

"Why are you so concerned about Moulan and her safeguarding the future?" he asked.

"I think it odd that you're not concerned."

Both boots were laced now. Between Delta's cynicism and Carcine's irony and that bomb that Rita dropped, I was swimming in an emotional abyss past the recesses of my mind. I am nothing that I thought I was and everything I hoped to be at the same time.

"Do you really think someone can hold your future? You think it's as simple as guarding a library?" he said. "Or maybe it's as simple as snatching a book?"

"So the Akashic Records aren't real?" I asked.

"I didn't say that," Delta said.

"Are the Tigers real?" I asked.

"You need to fight something, don't you? What's a rebellion without an enemy?"

But Delta's sarcasm was secondary to his preoccupation with the red feather he let dance in is hand. He was, it appeared, in his own world, transfixed by the innocence of the feather. The feather was dagger size. The blood-red color was as eye-catching as it was dangerous. I walked toward Delta and I too felt an energy radiating from it. He handed it to me. I held the stem and rotated it slowly. As broad as a quill pen, I had the feeling that this delicate beauty was so much more. I brushed my hand along its spine, and it elongated. I brushed my hands in the opposite direction, and it shrunk to thimble size. I flicked my wrist, and it morphed into a fan. I flicked it again, and it returned to its feather origins. "This was mine?" I said, half asking, half knowing. But no memories came to mind. Now I was in my own world.

I sat on the floor and crossed my legs. In my mind, I was back in the Crystal Cove, back to the safety of peace and wisdom, back to the all-knowing power of light. I felt the glow of a presence I could never articulate. I dug into my satchel and pulled out my book. I flipped through to an open page and held the feather in my hand. For some reason, I felt like the feather would morph into a pen; write a story of some sort. I held it in my hand, but nothing happened. I closed the book shut. The feather was a little too delicate to slip into the bag. I pulled a twisted bark string from my hair and hooked it around the feather. It was easier to adorn it than risk it getting crushed in my satchel. In the flip of a thought, I was back in Delta's Lair.

"I'm off to see Moulan," I said. "I assume you're not coming with me."

"You're gonna have to do this one on your own. But I'm always with you," he said, pointing to the turquoise necklace on his neck."

"How comforting," I said.

"You don't know everything, Rayla Illmatic."

No kidding, I thought. I shook my head and headed out the door.

Chapter 18

Life Where the Sky Ends

I hadn't visited Moulan since Carcine chose to vanish. The event was just days ago, but the sting and her likely involvement in it all kept me away. I needed time to reflect. I entered Moulan's parlor. Her door was always open, but the luster that made it magical the first go-round was gone. The staircase wasn't polished. The sparkling hues of green that shaded every wall and chair were speckled with dark blue dust.

"Hello," I said. My voice bounced off the walls.

She wasn't here. Odd, I could return later. As I turned to head for the door, I remembered Rita's charge.

"Get my book and I'll get you into Shogun City."

I dashed for the library, running from aisle to aisle until I found the golden shelf for R. Ritzy, Rehova, Regina, Roxanne, Rosarita, the shelf for R ran for miles. I didn't have much time, or did I? Rita of Harlem, Earth 1978; Rita of Acapulco 1499. There were at least a billion Ritas; and as I ran my fingers along the binding of each one, I felt like I was intruding. These were the lives and memories of billions of people, none of whom expected their every thought and lifetime to be etched in a database for all to access. Moulan's so-called safeguarding wasn't fair, and I must be careful not to read or in any way alter someone else's path.

It's much harder finding someone else's book. After scanning a glut of Ritas, I stopped. This was not a part of the mission. Just then, a gust of wind blew my loosely fastened feather from my hair and floated onto a nearby shelf. That's when I saw it, a soft pink book with silver trim. It read, Rita of Obama City. I flipped it open and saw Rita's dark eyes staring back at me. I tucked the book in my bag, grabbed my feather, and ran softly back for the hallway.

83

But Moulan had not returned. I scanned the perimeter, walking about the foyer, my boots clanked with every step; and that's when I heard it, the hum. Choruses of people were humming, a chant or a meditation maybe? I followed the hypnotizing hum to an adjacent leafy green hallway lined with life-size portraits of Moulan and shuddered when I saw black clouds of smoke billowing from a hole in the floor. I treaded slowly at first, but the stares from Moulan's eerie portraits made me walk faster. I spotted a mirror at the end of the hall and caught my breath when, for a second, my reflection resembled Moulan's. I fell to my knees and looked into the hole.

"Moulan," I said softly. She didn't answer. The hum grew louder. I reached into the pit and felt around until my hands grabbed the rung of a ladder. The smoke didn't choke me, and I assumed there was no fire below. I climbed into the pit. With each step, I swallowed fear. The hum grew louder. Eventually, my next step was my last. I fell a short distance to the floor, and a short round-faced man wearing a colorless shirt tripped over me.

"Watch it," he shouted. "And where's your uniform?" he snarled, before running off, a stack of papers clutched under his pudgy arm. A few more people darted past me, their eyes to the ground. At the end of the hall, a small crowd had gathered. Each wore colorless frocks, and they were hovering over something. I joined them, trying to nudge between and see what all the fuss was about. I pushed through just enough to see a glowing light-pink crystal lodged in the ground. "Color," one of them whispered. Just as I lifted my foot to take a step closer, a woman in a floor-length colorless skirt and grey box-shaped hat stood squarely in front of me. The angry green eyes said it all.

"Up the manhole," Moulan screeched through her teeth. And up we climbed. The others didn't notice us at all.

Chapter 19

Who's Aiming At My Pedestal?

BACK at Moulan's parlor, the missing charm that kept the place enchanted returned with our arrival. But no amount of glitter and sparkle could shake the dreariness of that city of no color. Suddenly, I felt as if I hadn't prepared properly. I kept the satchel tucked close, not sure how I could hold on to something that wasn't mine. I wanted to find Delta and ask him about these people before hearing Moulan's halfhearted explanation. But more time was the last thing I needed. I felt alone, still wounded from the revelation of my missing past and a bit dazed by this underground grey city. But Moulan promised to answer everything after she showered. Wearing no color made her ill, she chimed. Maybe this was a mistake, I thought. Just as I turned to slip out of her grasp, Moulan came descending down the staircase.

"There you are," she said, floating step by step as if she hadn't seen me just moments earlier. Her rich green gown flowed to her ankles, fluttering like a bird with the easy sway of her hips and thin waist. A bloom of ruffles at her collar elongated her neck. Her tresses were weaved into a bird's nest, an elaborate crown of coils atop her regal head. She'd even lined her eyes with green paint. Her insistence on elegance in these strangest of circumstances, I can at least respect. The frivolity would be laughable, but these times are not. "Tea?" she asked. I agreed. It was the only way to get a halfway straight answer. I nodded and we headed to the adjacent dining room. Moulan has prepared a feast of some sort. The spread of cakes, meats, and spreads were salivating,

"Just a little something I whip up for the soldiers. Anna, Enuk, and Scotch have such large appetites." Anna and Fajah ... I hadn't spoken to either since our return from East Africa. I felt a twinge of guilt for my selfishness. So much to do, so little time.

"Who were those people in the tunnel?" I asked.

"How was Rita?" she said, handing me a carrot muffin on a saucer.

The false pretense of pleasantries that Moulan enforced with the gentility of one of those funny Earth fables was the perfect backdrop for her bizarre tales. Ice made sure that those silly stories from Earth, the ones about giants and bean stalks, kid-eating witches, wars between stars, and pretty women rescued by men with nooses around their necks were archived in Planet Hope's museum. Puzzling stories, but enchanting.

"She asked about you."

"Nice feather," she said, sliding a plate of vegetables my way. The feather dangled from my hair, and Moulan avoided looking at it directly. Maybe she had an aversion to red. Surely, she must sense that I have the book. Something about its possession made me feel powerful. Was my power growing? Moulan busied herself, running to and fro, and she poured tea and passed cakes. Finally she took her seat.

"Rita can't have her book," she said plainly. "I know she wants it and I know she wants it very badly, but I'm not finished with my work. We must find the Missing." Why, I wondered, would a woman who had captured the future fear anything? Moulan, it seemed, had more enemies than she could count. "I'm not worried about the Shangos or Rita," she said. "I'm worried about you. You have powers you don't understand and people who want access to you. This, I feel is your only safe space. Here or the other lives you visit."

"You're afraid that I'll go to Shogun City," I added. "Was that grey place Shogun City?"

"Heavens no, Shogun City is much ritzier than that colorless swamp," she laughed, her hands flying up wildly. She knocked over her tea cup.

"Afraid of you going to Shogun City?" she said, breaking off a cookie and popping it in her mouth. She munched and continued talking as she flipped through napkins. "The thought never crossed my mind," she said, wiping away the spill with a silk napkin.

"You sent the Tigers didn't you?" I said. "Was it Rita you were after or me?"

"Don't be ridiculous. I would never reach out to the Tigers," she said.

"Do you think that little of me?"

"The Tigers vanished before my eyes," I added

"Really?" she said. I explained what I saw, and Moulan's nervous smile turned upside down.

But she did alert Cheyenne or at least Cheyenne's double. What was going on here?

"Whose side are you on?" I asked.

"Look, my beloved muffin, you have to stay focused. Once we find the Missing, all of this will be resolved."

"The Missing are your bartering chip, but for what?" I asked. "What have you done?" Moulan's green eyes were flaming fireballs. She slammed her tiny fist on the table, and the room shook. Moulan's genteelness couldn't take the challenge of inquisition. "They can't find the Crystal Cove!" she screamed. "You must not, whatever you do, allow them to get near the Crystal Cove. Nor can they protect this library. They will destroy everything. Everything!"

Moulan leaned back into her chair, exacerbated, as if she had shared something she's kept hidden for some time. They? For the longest time, "They" referred to our enemies. But Moulan wasn't talking about Dirk or the Tigers. Was she referring to the Originals? "The Dirk and his Tigers are just one problem," said Moulan. "But the Originals long to run the world, too." She sighed, her hot eyes melting with the fragility of our world. "Planet Hope is supposed to be a place of harmony, but both these 'too smart for their own good' teams have their own plans. Neither is best for the people," she said.

"Then let the people decide," I said. "Let us fight."

"Fighting. Isn't that what you called yourself doing for the last 75 years. Oops, I mean three years," she grinned, her smile too tightly wound to be pleasant. "You've been in hiding and fighting in the forest. You have no idea what's going on on this planet. No clue about the real peril. Everyone you know is in the Rebellion. You know nothing about the other people on Planet Hope. Think about it. Have you ever seen people, other than your friends or those dreaded Tigers on your warpath? No you have not."

I hadn't seen people, new people besides the ones in the tunnel, in some time. But I figured between the fighting and the hiding there wasn't time to befriend anyone. We were forbidden from engaging with anyone outside of the rebellion, largely because we didn't know whom to trust. While I hadn't met anyone, I do remember seeing people: the young boy with the overstuffed teddy bear in his hand and the yellow-hair who walked the narrow street on the edge of Obama City with his blue-haired mom; the man in the orange body suit with the tall green hat, who scurried by when I hid in the alleyway with Carcine in a battle waiting to pounce on a Tiger hold. But these images were so fleeting. They smelled of normalcy, a way of life my forest-trained lot couldn't embrace. I figured I'd simply erased the memories, but Moulan's beckoning emerald eyes made me wonder. Was the whole planet populated with Moulan-made doubles?

"When the Dirk began the mind tracking program, I tried to get the Originals to harbor the rest of the planet's citizens in Shogun City," Moulan said. "But between their rules and dogma and plain fear, they refused; but they were allowed into an underground suburb, if you will, called Sebastian's Cave. One by one, we slipped families into the cave. The conditions aren't the best, but at least they're safe. I created doubles to keep Dirk's Tigers at bay. "Doubles," I said. The word echoed in my head. Queasiness overcame me, but I swallowed it back down into the pit of my stomach.

"I created doubles of almost everyone. These doubles live and function, but they are not real.

"You didn't tell Rita until—," I said.

"Until after it was done," Moulan continued. "I didn't tell any of the Originals. By the time they found out, all of Planet Hope's citizens were safely tucked away."

"Does Dirk know?" I asked.

"I'm sure he suspects that something's wrong. But he was never a quick study."

Moulan had created Cheyenne's double, too.

"You held Rita hostage?" I said.

"It was for her own good," she shouted. She cracked her neck, easing her own stress. "For my own good." She giggled, grabbed a fan and flicked it rapidly in her face.

We sat in silence. Moulan's twists and turns were made with the best of intentions, but the hell she created was ours to bear. When life was restored, Moulan would surely be outcast. Maybe the Dirk was on to something when he deemed her enemy of the state. Her power was too great for her to handle responsibly, and now we were all paying for it.

"If the doubles are under your command, then we can end the war today," I said. Surely, the doubles could be reprogrammed to fight the Dirk or usurp those vanishing Tigers. Vanishing Tigers, I still couldn't reconcile this invisible fighting army with the peril of our land. What did Delta mean when he said we needed something to fight? "We have to find the Missing," she said cavalierly before sipping her tea with one dainty finger in the air. I'd had enough.

"The Missing you need to be concerned about are underground. You've lost the Neo Astronauts, you created doubles, and you've kidnapped time. Free the people in the cave," I said, banging my fist on the table. The plates and tea-cups rumbled. Now I was angry.

"I will not. They are being protected. The moment they come above ground, the Dirk will seize their mind."

"So you didn't end the Dirk's mind control," I said. "You just sent every-one to the cave? You tricked Rita. What about the doubles, what are they doing?"

"Living their lives," she said flatly.

"When the war ends, what will happen to them?"

"They will be terminated. Don't look at me like I created this mess. I am a protector. You want to save the world; find the Missing and all will be restored."

"Do I have a double?" I asked.

"No."

"Does Delta?" I asked.

"What difference does it make?"

"So some of the Originals have doubles, too? No wonder they hate you."

"It was the only way to keep them in check. No one threatens me. No one threatens to end my programs. The research is too valuable, the work too important. And I will not be ruled by a zealous group of elitists who want to re-work science for their own egalitarian purposes. No government, no fanatics, no one tells me what to do. Planet Hope will be free. The New-age astronauts are the galactic protectors of that freedom. Finding them is our only hope. "

But Planet Hope's destiny wasn't Moulan's decision alone. I felt her pain. I felt her craving to outwit the wittiest, to see further than the greatest seers, all for the noble cause of preserving our planet. She had been stretched beyond her own limits, crafting the next step, usually light-years ahead of everyone else. Despite her time hijinks, our planet was on the brink of destruction.

"Give me the book," she screamed. I pulled out my red feather, which flashed into a glowing sword. Moulan pulled out a hairpin that elongated into a double-edged one and our swords crossed with all the fury we could muster. She levitated, and I crouched in Tiger position.

"You do not know who I am," she shrieked.

"Likewise," I said.

We fought. Every movement of my body, every blow was devoted to her destruction. This game had gone on long enough. Moulan's force was heavy; and yet, I felt empowered. Her piercing shriek rang with every blow. I was angry, too. I blocked and lunged. But neither of us could throw the other off her stance. It was as if our strikes were meaningless. Just as I realized this, Moulan dropped her arms and started laughing. She whooped, she hollered, she belly laughed. I kept my fighting stance, waiting for her next move. When her sword shrunk to hairpin size, she reassembled her knotted locks and pinned them in a bun. I was struck with a revelation. There was no reality to a fight in a virtual world. I had no energy to waste. No real air to breathe. Fighting Moulan here was pointless. This was her world. I eased my stance.

"Anger will not help you here, sweet stuff," she said. "Keep the book," she said. "A gift from me to you."

"You can't outrun fate?" I said, catching my breath.

Moulan narrowed her eyes and looked down her nose.

"Honey, I am fate," she replied.

A knock at the door broke her stare.

"It is time," said Moulan. Delta entered; he looked from Moulan to me. I stood disheveled, panting lightly, my tightly gripped sword at my side. Moulan flitted about as if nothing had happened.

"There are the Tigers, there are the Originals and there's us," Moulan reminded me, as if we hadn't warred with one another seconds earlier. "We keep it in the balance. Find the rest of the Missing." Moulan walked out, her head lifted as if she was commanding us to follow. Delta moved quickly behind her. I didn't move at first anyway. Moulan was the fragile link holding this mess of a world together. I trusted her because I had to. But I always have choice.

Delta and I followed Moulan into her chamber. A grand piano sat in the middle of the room. A portrait-sized mirror was the only wall adornment. Moulan lifted her skirt, sat at the bench before the monster instrument, and danced her fingers up and down the pale green keys. Black and white photos of a woman and two men sat atop the piano in golden frames. I hadn't heard music in some time, and the majesty of the notes had me spinning. My shoulders relaxed and I swayed with the melody. "Diva, Lagos and Dexter," Moulan sang in a register so high, I almost covered my ears. "Study their faaaaces." I took Delta's hand and swung myself around. Confused, he smiled and we danced and danced. When Moulan stopped playing, day had turned into night and finally I was able to nap on the cold wood floor.

According to Moulan, Diva, Lagos, and Dexter were in 1971 America. They were part of some kind of militant group that fought for human rights, she said, similar to our rebellion. While they were leaders in their group, they were outsiders in the city; and Delta and I would need to find them and bring them home. They're highly skilled, but they are known for their intellect, their ability to strategize, and their ample communication skills. They are also unusually skilled in the martial arts. The threesome was in a dead heat on a mission of their own. Delta and I would be outsiders in their world; but we, together, would have to get to know them.

"Where are we going?" Delta asked.

"To Washington D.C," she said. "It is the capital of the nation."

"You will be carrying something very, very important; and it is critical that you bring that item back with you. Don't ask what it is. I honestly don't know."

"And when we return, then what?" I asked.

"Then you'll go back for the rest," she said. "You and Delta will share a love for space travel. It will dominate your thoughts; it will push you into the unknown."

"A theme," I quipped. Moulan ignored me. But it was clear to both Moulan and Delta that I was in no way focused enough for aural travel. I needed an anchor, something to bring me back.

For a brief moment, I yearned for the comforts of the Enchanted Forest. I longed for the circle of the Sisterhood, who protected me from these wild dimensions I now treaded through. I yearned for the wise words of Sui Lee, my caretaker and teacher. She would know what to do. She, above all else, loved humanity and fought fiercely to protect our rights as beings on this world. Her motherly love saw me through the worst of times. Because of her, I was alive today. In a flash, I saw her, an image of Sui Lee, legs crossed in a haze of grey. The vision left as quickly as it came. Sui Lee is alive.

"I want to go to Sebastian's Cave," I said.

Moulan wrinkled her nose. "As you wish," said Moulan, her voice heavy with defeat. In the blink of an eye, a manhole appeared in the floor. Moulan stuck the heel of her boot in a groove in the circular lid and flicked it aside. The metal cover clanked as it fell. Black smoke bellowed from the underworld. "Delta, please accompany her," she said, before wrinkling her nose and floating off.

Chapter 20

See You When the Clock Ticks

DELTA and I climbed down The Bottomless Ladder. It felt like I'd been snaking down this narrow hole for hours, but Delta claimed it was no more than 15 minutes, not that time seemed to matter much anymore. Delta was above me, I was below him, and he wasn't comfortable with our setup. The hole was pitch black; and with every step down the rung, I prayed that I'd reach the bottom. Eventually I did.

A sea of cave dwellings and tents engulfed us. A string of people purposely zipped through the labyrinth of homes. Women drug little kids along. Men darted among them. Delta and I might as well have been invisible. Then I felt a tug on my arm. A little round-faced boy with dark eyes and freckles stared back at me.

"Hello," he said. "Are you a visitor?"

"You could say that," I added.

"You're from Shogun City," he chimed. "Is the war over?" he asked.

"What do you know about the war?" I asked.

"I know that Shogun City will rise and that the Neo Astronauts will come to save us. Obama City lives. Planet Hope will be restored." I was startled.

"My name is Doug," the boy said, extending his hand, and I shook it firmly.

"I'm Rayla, Rayla Illmatic."

The boy gasped. *"The Illmatic,"* he whispered. "You're the daughter of Illmatic. They hid you in Shogun City, and you became the greatest warrior they ever had and then ..... Is that Delta Blue!"

"Doug," a small, thin woman with a pointed nose shrieked before snatching the young boy away. The two fled off through the towering teepees and disappeared.

"Rayla, in here," Delta bellowed. Standing next to a black teepee, he opened the flap and lowered his head to enter. I followed.

Inside, a woman sat with her legs crossed. Her back was to me. Her long black ponytail brushed the floor. Her build was slight, but strong. I know this woman could it be—"Hello Rayla," she said. It was Sui Lee. I stepped toward her, tears welling from my eyes.

"Don't," she said. "It won't help either of us. Stay where you are."

Delta grabbed my arm I snatched away. He stepped out of the tent to leave us alone.

"My beloved, Rayla. I'm sorry that I left you. But I came because the people need light. They need love. I am the only one left from the Enchanted Forest. I'm here to remind them of who they are to restore hope."

I fell to my knees.

"Everyone knows who they are but me."

"Blame helps no one. I chose to be here. Just like you chose to see me."

I cried. I cried because I was tired of this song and dance. Tired of this web of discovery, tired of the confusion that had become my life. I felt Sui Lee's warm fingers message my scalp, and I buried my head in her chest.

"We need you to push on," Sui Lee said. "I made sure that you learned amongst the best, because so much of our progress depends on you. I'm counting on you. Moulan's counting on you, and so are the astronauts."

"Why does everything depend on me?" I asked, my voice cracking with sorrow.

"Because this is your story."

I looked up, but she turned away.

94

"You're doing just fine," she said. "You've learned so much, but there is so much more for you to do. We all have our role to play. For now, I must stay with our people. Go now. I'll be right here."

"I love you, Sui Lee."

"I love you, too."

I kissed the back of her head, pushed myself off the floor. Sui Lee returned to her meditation. I took one last look at her dangling pony tail and left.

Outside the tent, I surveyed the colorless clad people, running to and fro. For a split second, I wondered if Carcine was amongst them. Probably not. I shook off the thought, tapped Delta on the shoulder and headed for the ladder. The route to the top was much quicker than the climb down. It happens like that sometimes. I felt empty, like a bottomless vessel. Yet I was as drained as I was empowered. I thought of nothing as I climbed, gripping the cold iron rungs instead.

Before we pushed the manhole open, Delta stopped me. "Are you sure that you don't want to go to Shogun City first?" he asked. "I know how to get there from here."

It hadn't dawned on me that Delta knew of Sebastian's Cave, too. I did want to go to Shogun City. Every fiber of my being longed for my missing past. But I remembered Sui Lee's words. "Push forward." And somehow, I felt that a trip to Shogun City would keep me from finding the astronauts. I feared that what I would discover would keep me there, bound by the mystery of the past. And yet, my push forward was taking me to another past, a much more distant one. Somehow, I felt that this life in 1971 America held the key to unlocking something deep within my soul, something I would need once I arrived in Shogun City. I felt that what I would learn in 1971 America would put me in touch with this mystery gift both Moulan and Rita talked about. "We must push forward, Delta," I said and flipped the lid of the manhole so hard, it crashed like a thunderbolt to the floor. I would go to sleep in Delta's Lair, and in the morning, we would teleport to Earth.

***

"Diva, Lagos, and Dexter," I said. Moulan was mixing a blue substance in a jar. I sat in a wooden high chair beside Delta. I could see their faces in my mind. I could feel their fire. This mission would be very different from the last.

"They won't be as cooperative, will they?" I said.

"I can tell you the facts and nothing else," snapped Moulan.

I rubbed the turquoise necklace that sat coolly on my chest.

95

Moulan poured her concoction into two silver thimbles and handed one to me and one to Delta. The necklace we shared was glistening on Delta's neck. I thought of Carcine and his numbing absence. I didn't care to see him this go-round, although I felt for a second that he longed to see me. "On the count of three," she said. "One, two—," but I'd already doused the drink down. I had been down the rabbit hole just moments before. There was nothing to fear.

Chapter 21

Eyes Open When Shut

THE fluorescent light in the women's bathroom at the military barracks wasn't flattering at all. My brown skin looked muted with a haze of green in this awful light. Fortunately, my hair had grown some while I was away, and I picked it out into the blowouts everyone was wearing these days. Not bad, I figured. The story was that I had been honorably discharged, but I suggested ditching the uniform for the interview. Something simple: jeans, a green turtle neck, and a simple leather jacket should be enough. But I didn't get clearance for the red feather earring. When my supervisor saw me exit the bathroom with the feather dangling, he just shook his head. "Make it good," he said before dipping off into the next room.

The doors shut behind me. I walked down the white hallway alone; through the glass I could see the reporter waiting for me. A tall guy in a tan cotton trench, he walked alongside me, the thick glass as our divider. He planned to question me as soon as the hallway door flew open. Everyone loves a hero. The problem was, I wasn't one. "Bettye Love," he shouted as I came out of the hallway. Bettye Xavier Love was my name today, but I'd go by Bettye X for short. My superiors figured that if I was promoted as a hero, I'd get more access, meet more people, and I could get the scoop on some of the subversive activities popping up all over the place. Didn't make a heap of sense really, made me too visible. But this was their game, not mine.

The story was that I was a POW, a prisoner of war in Vietnam. The reality: I was an undercover agent, disguised as an army nurse, planted to get as much info on a place called the Crystal Cove, some underground maze of crystals that all sides wanted, but none could find. Like the fabled fountain of youth, men had lost their senses on the quest for this magical place located somewhere in the marshes of southeast Asia. Some thought its discovery could give us an edge in the war. The crystals were a rich mineral source, but they were also rumored to have mystical powers, and some soldiers had stories of finding crystals that healed their injuries. One soldier confided that his platoon was ambushed; and while ducking for cover, he stumbled over a giant pink crystal. He placed both hands on it, a force field of sorts surrounded the battalion, and the bombs and bullets bounced off like rubber bands. The men tried to dig it up and take it with them, but couldn't rip the thing out the ground. I was gathering these stories, talking to wounded men about what they saw and trying to pinpoint the source of these mysterious rocks. But no one ever reclaimed anything tangible. One night, our base was raided. I sustained multiple injuries, but threw enough grenades to keep the enemy at bay. I crawled into the moss for cover and fell into a pit, a mysterious cave. I had found the Crystal Cove all right; but the question was, would anyone find me.

It was the most beautiful sight I'd ever seen, a natural array of rainbow-colored crystals sparkling like jewels in the sky. For the first time in my life, I felt a shared bond with nature, a mutual love, as if these powerful rocks and I were one. I marveled at the wonder, unable to detach myself from the captivating beauty of it all. And the sense of peace that overcame me was like nothing I'd ever felt before. At one point, I just sat, legs crossed, mesmerized by the dancing lights and colors and the wondrous symbols they formed circling my head like a halo. I couldn't leave; I didn't leave, for what seemed like three days.

Although I had no food, I was replenished. I don't know how I got out. All I remember is running on the beach white sand, flagging down choppers, and Blue running out to greet me. I had grabbed a few crystals with me. The troops said that I had saved the base. I don't know how. They had some wild story of me doing hand-to-hand combat with the enemy, rescuing them and restoring them to health. The next night, they said, the enemy returned and I was captured. I remembered none of it. All I remembered was sitting in the cave mesmerized by the crystals of life.

"How long have I been gone?" I asked Blue, as I huddled in the back of the chopper.

"Nine months," he replied.

I believed none of it. Psychologists questioned me and doctors poked and prodded; and while they concluded that I was of sound mind, the details of my disappearance were totally up in the air.

Some figured I had been captured and leaned on my imagination to make light of solitary confinement. The conspiracy nuts speculated that I had slipped into some kind of time portal. All I knew was that for a moment, I had experienced a peace that transcended this world. And the radiance from those crystals of light would stay with me forever. Whatever the case, I was given a Purple Heart.

My superiors were pleased with the fact that I'd at least recovered a few pink crystals, and they were studying it night and day in labs to no avail. They couldn't find anything special about them, and the dismal results made me nervous. What happened to me out there? But they told me to relax a bit and started yapping about me being a war hero; something some 35 troops could testify to and I couldn't remember.

One of the crystals, a bright turquoise one, I kept for myself —a fact I chose not to share. It was tucked away in the lining of my brown satchel. But I couldn't tell that to the reporter who greeted me in the hall either. He wouldn't understand my meditative time warp any more than I did. An enthusiastic guy, who worked for a black newspaper, he was granted the story of the hometown hero. He would break the news, a community marketing ploy, and the big papers would follow. As for my story, my superiors told me to lie low on the crystal bit and drilled me on the details of heroic efforts I couldn't recall as well as some canned responses about my supposed captivity. In my supervisor's excitement for having given some credence to the Cove story, he forgot to drill me of what the details of my fictitious hometown story would be.

As I recalled, I think this go-round I was a military brat from southwest DC, with a dad who had fought in the Korean War—no other family. At least this story was part true. I was raised by my dad, but he was a janitor. He had majored in physics in the 40s, but labs weren't hiring black men then; so he worked as a janitor at a top university, reading all he could and tinkering on his projects into the wee hours of the night. A man living with a broken heart, he passed away when I was young, and I was raised in an orphanage outside DC. But I had an affinity for science, and one of our well-intentioned headmasters recommended me to a spy scout, who visited the orphanage looking for possible recruits. I was so wide-eyed and cute, they said, that no one would suspect me of anything. The reporter didn't need to know that either.

"I'm Carcine Blackfoot," the reporter, said shaking my hand vigorously. "Should we do the interview here?" he asked. I surveyed the sterile white room and cold metallic table and walked out the door. I needed air. He followed. I found a rickety bench near a patch of shady oaks by a river. I took one end and he took the other. He slid down towards me, fumbling a bit as he reached for a recorder in his brown briefcase. A tall, broad-shouldered man with wavy black hair that dusted his shoulders, he had the look of a black Clark Kent in disguise. His barreled chest was a little too big for his buttoned up white shirt; his football player thighs, a bit too muscular for his beige suit pants. He wore thick black-framed glasses, too. Maybe I wasn't ready for this assignment. I could not keep my mind from wandering.

The sunlight glistened off the water, and I thought of the Crystal Cove. This was my first real moment with regular people in a while. Although I'd prepped for this, I didn't realize how overcome I would be with normalcy. A young mother was pushing a stroller; others were dressed for work, darting back to lunch or a meeting. A few teenagers were riding bikes.

"What day is this?" I asked Carcine.

"Friday," he said.

Based on the angle of the sun, it had to be just after 12.

"And the time?"

"Uh, 12:30 pm. Bout lunch time.

"What month is this?" I asked, soaking in the sights.

"June, Ms. Love. It's June."

"Call me Bettye," I replied. Looks like the tape recorder wasn't working, so he dug back into his tattered briefcase and pulled out a yellow legal pad. Back to business.

"What's with that crazy integrating a Woolworth story you told my superiors about," I said. I was a kid when that stuff was happening.

"It was the best I could do," he offered. "We're both military brats, and when I found out your dad was from Richmond, like my dad, I figured I had a shot," he said. I didn't know who this guy was or how he passed through clearance, but I ran with it. I guess he was the ideal ploy for the story. I hoped this guy didn't ask me a bunch of questions about Richmond; I've never been to the place.

I told Carcine a riveting story, every bit of it a bold-faced lie as far as I was concerned, because I had no memory of it. But I had memorized the affidavits. I talked about torture, death-defying fights, night raids. He seemed like a good guy; and this story, I figured, would help what was surely a fledgling journalism career. He ate it up, lapping up my lies like a cat does milk.

"What a story," said Carcine. "So are you ready to tell me the truth?"

Suspicious fellow. I chuckled. "This is the best you're gonna get, Mister."

So he didn't believe it. Puzzling. Looks like I've got a live one. Usually,

I'd have my antenna up; but right now, I just enjoyed the sunshine, the laughter from the kids running in the distance, and the site of the city obelisk in clear view. It was a win-win as far as I was concerned. He got a hard-luck, dare devil story; and I got to satisfy my superiors. And he was cute. I seriously hope they don't make him a target.

"So what are you gonna do now?" he asked. "You lookin' for work? Going back to nursing?" Nursing? Oh, right, my cover. But it was so hard to focus. The monotony of everyday life was so magical. When was the last time I'd just sat and observed normal people?

"I'm fine," I said.

"The world's changed some since you've been away."

"The world is always changing," I retorted.

I'd read about the changes—the riots, the activism.

I didn't want to be a part of any of it. I wanted to buy a motorcycle and ride into the sky, til my next mission, anyway. Maybe I would sing rock songs and paint.

"This may sound funny, but, uh, I'm proud of you, Bettye. Everyone doesn't have what it takes to be a hero. Not in these times," he said.

It was the only real sentiment of care I'd heard since I returned. The only nugget of truth that rang right since I was stuck in the Cove. I want that radiant love back. He handed me a flyer. "It's a poetry reading, hosted by the Purple Angels Society. You have a love affair with words, thought you'd dig it. And I'll buy you a drink."

"A drink, now you're talkin'," I said.

Chapter 22

Moon Beams Tickle Me Funky

My apartment was tiny, which made the fact that I had to share it with Captain Blue for the next two weeks tantamount to hell. There was some mix-up in our housing, and the agency just put the two of us together Two smart-ass undercover agents in the same space. And the clock ticks. I was biding my time, waiting for this story to take off before they gave me an assignment, anyway. I adjusted my stockings, and folded the collar on my ribbed turtleneck. This Purple Angels Society had a ring to it. I was curious, but most importantly, I felt that I had to put Carcine at ease. My wilder than wild tale only confirmed in his mind that I was a spy. But then again, showing up would do the same thing. Oh well, I would have to throw off his scent, or at least create some doubt. The agency had been recruiting black spies for some time, and the revolutionaries feared that many were infiltrating their organizations, their sets. And we were. But tonight, I wasn't on a mission. I was hanging out in D.C.

Blue sat in a lounge chair and was sharpening his switchblades, which he had lined neatly on the coffeetable in the tiny living room we shared. Cooling out in his belled jeans and a black silk undershirt, he saw me primping in the bathroom mirror, hopped up and pulled the flyer from the mirror's edge.

"What do you know about them?" he asked?

"Nothing, "I said. "Just going to hear a little poetry."

"You know they're on the investigation list," he said.

"Why wouldn't they be, they're a bunch of aspiring radicals talking people power. Of course they're on the list. But these sets seem to be the only thing going on these days."

"You're not going out with that reporter are you?" he asked.

I'm always amazed by men who turn big brother on you.

"I don't recommend it," he added. "He's a little too curious if you ask me. He's a fast climber on the come-up. Did you check his background?"

"The agency checked it," I said, before gliding a blood-red tube of lipstick over my lips.

"But did you check it?" he asked. Some of us, on the low, were questioning the agency's mission as well. The stories of agents set up and left in the wind were mounting. Blue was one of those guys who wanted to be covered on all sides. I got it, but something happened to me in that Crystal Cove, and my world lens was not the same. Life took on new meanings beyond the self-preservation that Blue insisted on and beyond the agency's search to undermine enemies. "You need some air," I said, pushing past Blue and slamming the door behind me.

Chapter 23

SuperStar

A red-light hue lit the bar. Mack's Place was right by a train track. In fact, it rattled a bit every time a train passed by. Crowded and small, the scene these days was nothing but rebels, college kids, and poets. Mack, I assumed, was the bald, round guy with the double chin behind the bar.

"I need a pretty bartender like you," he whispered, sweat from his head gleamed under the dangling bar light. He slid me a shot glass of warm vodka. I downed it just as a lanky guy, almost too tall for this hole in the wall's low ceilings shoved a flyer in my face. Protect Yourself—Martial Arts for Self-Defense.

"You need this sista, more than you need this drink," he said, his gold tooth glowing. He weaved between the crowd, standing two heads taller than the tallest in the room. So they teach kung fu in the basement. Interesting.

There was a lot of pulsating testosterone in this place; and I was getting a little tired of pretty men telling me what to do, when Carcine slipped beside me, notebook in hand.

"Sorry I was late."

"Just don't do it again," I said. He passed me a clipboard, some sign-in list for poets. He looked at me, as if to dare me to sign it. Slots 2-8 were taken. I signed my name at the top of the list. Bettye.

The lanky guy came between us and collected the clipboard. His distinct features were reminiscent of the West African Dogon masks I saw at a tiny gallery in Paris. We had a layover in the city for a couple of days before we headed off to war. And our crackerjack-box-sided hotel was next door to an even smaller gallery, run by the son of a collector whose father travelled the world. The familiarity I saw in those masks is the same way I feel about too-tall Chuck. He looked from the board back to me and headed for the mike.

The lanky guy's name was Lagos, a nickname of his in tribute to his African past and the Nigerian city of the same name. Charismatic, but serious, he opened the reading with a pledge to liberty that all knew accept for me. "Ashe," he said, at the conclusion and the audience was the chorus to his Chiron.

"We'd like to welcome a newcomer to the stage. Welcome her into the fold." The group clapped politely. I snaked through the crowd. I waited for Lagos to hand me the mike, but he kept it in his grip.

"Tell us about yourself," he said, jamming the mike so close to my mouth, I might as well have swallowed it.

"I'm Bettye and I'm here to bless the mike."

"Where you from?"

"I'm just in that here and now."

"Give her the damn mike," someone yelled in the crowd.

"Respect," Lagos yelled, and a few people snickered.

He handed me the mike, not wanting to. A host with an attitude. I surveyed the crowd and began.

"People live the lie, cause the truth is a memory

People live the lie, cause the truth is a memory

When I remember who I was, I yearn to forget

But I remember to free the people

I am the people, I am the truth

And I slash through my lies, although I love the deception

I live for the air, and breathe for the breathless

A new me from the water does rise.

Truth reigns, Ashe."

105

The crowd erupted in applause. I snaked through the accolades and felt a familiar breath on my neck. "What the hell was that?" Delta whispered, gliding beside me and hiding his anger behind his sunglasses. This big brother stuff was really getting on my nerves. So he's following me.

"Get a life," I replied. I was tired of pretending. Tonight, I was gonna be me ... as much of me as I could afford to be.

I made my way to the bar, back to Carcine. "Let's get out of here," I told him. "People live the lie, cause the truth is a memory," Carcine repeated.

"Deep and heavy. Did you write that one in the war?" I grinned. We all get tired of lies. While I could never reveal my identity, I could lash out if I wanted to. Through the glow of well-wishers, I could feel the cold stare from the corner. Lagos was eying me.

"Don't mind him, he just likes checkin' cats out," whispered Carcine. There's rumors of a lot of deep-cover cats around, so he just wants to let everyone know he's righteous." I didn't see how cold-staring someone at a poetry reading would crack a case, but he's justified in being suspicious.

"What are the rumors?" I asked.

"Everything's so mixed up these days, hard to call a spade a spade. Friend of mine in Mississippi said you couldn't throw a rock without hitting an informant. The revolution is real, so the eyes are upon us."

That's for sure, I thought.

"Besides, everyone knows a female war hero is in town, and everyone's not so keen on vets. You stand out."

"So what are you lookin' to do?"

"I just want to write the story, document the change."

"What change?" I asked.

"The world's spinnin' fast. Just want to make sure our people are right side up when it's done. Document it for the history books."

His eyes were earnest, warm enough to melt a chilled heart. I leaned in and kissed him. I was so dazzled by the sweetness of it that I didn't feel the shadow that engulfed us. But a shadow came over us, literally. Standing at 6 feet each, a woman and a man, both in leather jackets stood before us.

"You Bettye X?" the guy asked.

I didn't respond.

"Of course it's her," Carcine said. "Bettye X in the flesh."

"I'm Dexter and this is Diva. Minister Lagos would like to have a word with you."

"Maybe tomorrow; I'm busy," I said, standing to leave. Carcine did the same.

"Leaving so fast," Lagos said. His voice was so deep it nearly rattled the glass window.

"Lagos, she's cool," Carcine interjected.

"It's all good," I told Carcine.

Lagos extended his hand, ushering me towards a door that led to a basement. Oh, this was going to be so fun. The door shut in Carcine's face.

We sat around a wooden table, one not too different from my debriefing table a few days earlier. And while the department hadn't given me a new assignment yet, this group of eager rebels would surely give me all the info I needed to prepare for the next. Observation number one in the spy game is that most people talk too much. They talk, tell you their damn life story, and then they don't listen. Those who don't talk give themselves away with gestures, acquaintances, clothing. I'm sure Delta spotted their moves and wasn't more than a few feet away from the basement door. But I won't need backup for this one. Diva spoke first.

"I'll get right to the point," she said. "We need someone to train us. We heard about your stint in the war; and since we're in a war of our own, we thought we should get some specialized training."

"You making a karate movie?" I said.

"You've been on the inside," Dexter said. "We need your insight." Dexter had the build of a strong man, but his tense shoulders were more like those of a hunched-over typist or research scientist than a fighter. Interesting.

"I can't share intelligence without jeopardizing my life," I added.

"Your life is already jeopardized," Lagos bellowed. "So we're willing to accommodate you." With that, Lagos pulled out a black velvet cloth, wrapped in a ball. He unfolded it, and I was blinded by the light. Diamonds, a handful of

107

diamonds. So this wasn't such a small-time operation after all.

"Nice," I said, inspecting the diamonds. "What do you need the training for?"

We can't tell you," Diva said firmly. She was, I assumed, the enforcer of the bunch. Her icy practicality was a dead ringer for a woman who knew how to operate explosives. I picked up the diamonds one by one. They were real. No fakes in this bunch. Flawless. Precision cut. How odd.

"What's your time frame?" I asked.

"We got six weeks," said Lagos.

"Give me a day or two to think about it," I said.

"We can't do that," said Dexter. "We can't give you that kind of time."

"It's either now or not at all," said Diva.

"Cool it, Diva," said Dexter, leaning forward in his chair and baiting my response. This was getting interesting.

"Or what?" I said.

"Or we reveal that Bettye X forgot where she came from," said Diva. "We know a two-bit orphan when we see one."

I stood and Diva reached for my arm. I twisted her and pushed her to the wall. Dexter yelled "Hey." Dexter ran toward me full speed; I dipped and landed a whopping blow to his back. He hit the floor. Lagos stared at me coldly, a smile creeping across his lips, the footsteps and Delta Blue's yell was all that saved him.

"Police, everybody up against the wall," Delta yelled. I snatched the diamonds off the floor. Lagos, Carcine, and I were at the wall. The other cops pulled Diva and Dexter off the ground. We all marched up the rickety steps. The others went with the local cops. I went in the car with Delta.

"What the hell was that?"

"They know who I am. I don't know why Captain gave me this war-hero rap. Makes me too damn visible."

"You don't need a picture in the paper to do that."

Delta made a hard left at the light and pulled in front of a white two-story warehouse, a replica of every other factory in this mostly deserted area.

"Welcome to paradise. It's our new setup."

"Our?" I said.

"I've been assigned to partner with you. They want us together."

Delta and I climbed the steps into our dugout, a large warehouse floor, sparse, with a few pieces of rickety furniture and two steel beds. I sat on steel bed number one, feeling the metal through the thin mattress. I pulled the bag of diamonds from my pocket. I replayed Diva's words, "forgot where I came from." Did I know her in the orphanage? I used to wonder what I would do if I bumped into another kid from the orphanage. Would they remember me? Was I tripping? Maybe she meant my cover. Delta stretched out on a battered brown leather couch and turned on the TV. The black and white image flickered, and Delta adjusted the metal hanger that doubled as the antennae. But the image was supposed to be grainy,

"They're back on the moon again," he said, falling back into his seat. "I need to scrap this intelligence jazz and join NASA."

"They don't want rogue agents up there," I chimed. "They need scientists."

"They need to militarize that piece before these other countries get there. That's what they need to do. Do you know the threat to national security that could pose? That could be a disaster." He was right, as usual. The astronaut life seemed like a peaceful option right about now. It was much more pleasant being one of two on the moon than contemplating the risk of a blown cover.

"They'll be in the slammer for a night or two," said Blue. "We figured public nuisance was better than a kidnapping charge. Then your cover would be blown for sure."

"They wanted to pay me to train them," I said.

"For what?"

"Didn't say."

"Thanks to you, now we have to find out." Delta went to the makeshift refrigerator and pulled out a beer, he handed one to me. So much for my night out. I didn't mention Diva and the orphanage to Delta. I dubbed them the Lost Years; and besides the higher-ups in the agency itself, no one knew how I slipped into this world of espionage. I didn't like talking about it. Instead, Delta and I sat sprawled out on the couch, listening to the TV broadcast on the moon landing. I wonder if I'd make a good astronaut. I turned to ask Delta, but he'd fallen asleep. Just as I was nodding off with visions of spacesuits in my head, a white light hit our window pane.

Delta popped up. We looked at one another. He ducked behind a curtain on the wall and looked down.

"Your boyfriend's calling. That kid's not gonna make it."

"He must have followed us," I said.

"Not good," Delta pulled out his gun from the small of his back and hid behind the glare of the window.

"I knew something was up with him."

Yeah, but the control unit cleared him. He's just nosy."

"No one is just nosy," added Delta.

We looked at one another. Was Carcine an agent, too? Was he assigned to watch us? But that clumsy flashlight screamed inexperience.

Knock, knock, knock. Delta slipped into the next door and nodded for me to open.

"Who is it?"

"Carcine. Bettye is that you?"

I opened the door and whisked him in, slammed him against the wall, and patted him down. No weapons, no wires.

"Hell of a greeting," he said.

"Carcine, what are you doing here?"

"I followed you. What happened down there?"

I went to the fridge and handed him a beer." He took a seat on the thin couch and looked about. I sat in the chair across from him. He was earnest, bold, and naïve. He wanted a Pulitzer or to crack some big case, believing that one dent in the system could change the world. He's a believer. I wanted to believe in change, too. I wanted out of this mess. I wanted the Crystal Cove.

"You want something and you've wanted it since you faked that inter-view," I reasoned. "Shoot." He pulled a folded newssheet from his pocket. It had a photo of my father.

"Your dad was my mentor," he said.

"Enough of this," screamed Delta, who bolted from the other room and steam-rolled into Carcine. But Carcine flipped him to the ground, pinning him, snatching the gun from his hand. I didn't intercede. I didn't move.

"Don't move one inch, Bettye," said Carcine. "I'm not going to hurt you. Either of you." Dammit. Who was this man?

"Just as I suspected," he said. "You're both agents. Well that mystery is solved. You can come in now," Carcine shouted. Lagos, Diva, and Dexter sauntered in, surveying the warehouse that was our temporary abode. Carcine had Delta pinned to the floor.

"Let him up," I told Carcine. I came to Delta's aid, not that he needed it. Although I could have wacked all four of them, something told me to just cool it and listen. I whispered to Delta.

"Hear them out," I said. "And don't make any sudden moves. They're friends."

"Friends, my ass," whispered Delta. Lagos, Diva, and Dexter circled the room. They felt safe for the moment and took posts around the room.

"Now that we're all here we can speak honestly," said Carcine.

"My high school teacher reached out to your dad to tutor me in science. They thought I might go to college. And because of him, I did. But your dad was an inventor. I've been building on his work ever since. That's why I came to find you."

"Don't believe him, Bettye," Delta shouted. But I ignored him.

"Go on," I said.

"We've been working on a new invention: a technology, an information portal where you can store and transfer information and messages in the air.

"Store a message in the air?" I said, "Like a telephone?"

"Or a TV signal," said Carcine. "We've been experimenting with it, sending messages back and forth. But we've been getting these crazy messages, as if someone's using our technology to communicate back; but we can't decode, and we were hoping that you could help us."

"Why would we be able to help you?" I asked.

"Because you've been to the Crystal Cove," he said. "The troops I interviewed said it's all you talked about."

111

Lagos interjected. "We were hoping that you'd brought some back with you, or at least, you could get access to them."

"Why?" I asked.

"Because they hold messages, and they—or it—are trying to communicate with us."

Where were these people getting their information from?

"Anything that she knows is classified information," said Delta. "And we don't owe you …."

"Let me see your invention," I said.

"Your dad believed in using crystal-based technology as a communication device. It's all he worked on," said Carcine. I didn't know what my father was working on all those years. I never thought to wonder. The others were looking for my response. I took a seat and they all did the same.

Lagos pulled out a large watch out of one pocket, and two stone-sized diamonds out of a velvet bag in the other. He sat the watch in between the two diamonds on the small wooden coffeetable, and a triangle of light formed. Delta and I perked up in our chairs. He nodded to Dexter. Dexter moved to the other side of the room and set up a duplicate contraption. A triangle of light formed above it, too.

"The watch has letters on it," says Lagos." "And when I type a message, the word 'hi,' morphed in lights inside of Dexter's triangle."

Dexter typed something and the word "Hello" popped up in Lagos triangle.

"We were testing this out for a couple of months, and then one day, these symbols popped up in the triangle. Neither of us was typing a thing. Diva pulled out a rumpled notebook and handed it to me.

Yes, I'd seen these symbols before. I spent nine months in the cove, studying the stones, meditating. As for the symbols, they were engraved all over the cave. These symbols and those mysterious rocks were my friends. They saved me. I shook it off.

"Yes, I've seen these words. But I don't know what they mean."

"We cross-referenced it with other symbols—Egyptian, Berber, Sumerian, Chinese. No similarities."

"It's older than all of them. No one speaks this language anymore," I said.

"Or maybe it hasn't been spoken before," said Lagos.

"We think it's coming from the future."

I looked to the triangle and saw the letters I L L M A T I C.

"What is that word?" asked Diva.

"Do you have any of the stones?," asked Carcine.

I was looking at the letters. Slowly the letters dissipated and my eyes jetted to the TV screen to the men on the moon.

"Bettye."

I grabbed my bag and ripped the blue crystal out the lining, tossing it to Carcine.

"You don't need it, though. You have everything you need. Excuse me."

I walked over to the bathroom and shut the door. I threw cold water in my face and looked into the mirror. I saw myself the real me. My name was Rayla Redfeather. I remember her; I remember her in the Cove. I remember and then it all went black.

I opened my eyes. Delta, Dexter, Carcine, and Diva were standing above me. I sat up slowly.

"We have to go," I said.

"Go where?" asked Carcine.

I looked to the flickering TV screen. "To the moon. We have to go to the moon."

Delta grabbed my arm. "Why don't we rest for a while?"

"No, we have to leave now." I ran for the door and the others ran behind me. Carcine stayed behind. I guess he wanted to tell the story. We had to get out of here, but it was too late. As soon as I stepped out the door, the floodlights were upon us. Two choppers circled in the air. Several squad cars surrounded us.

But it didn't matter, I am Rayla Redfeather. I am Illmatic.

"Put your hands in the air," an officer shouted through his megaphone.

"I am Rayla Redfeather," I shouted. "Take my hand," I screamed, the others, puzzled, just did what I said.

"Look to the moon."

"I said put your hands in the air," an officer repeated.

I looked for the Crystal Cove amongst the hints of grey spotting our planet's moon. I did not see it, but I would be there soon.

"Look up. Hurry now," I told the others. Blue and Lagos looked to me, and all lifted their eyes to the black skies. "I am Rayla Redfeather," I cried. A shooting star streaked the sky, right in front of the full moon that hung above us. The flash of light blinded us all. If only I could take the Crystal Cove with me.

Chapter 24

Firm on Foreign Land

THE soft rap of knocks on the door felt like a thud on my head. "You're up," said Moulan, floating in with her plate of cookies. She put her hand under my chin and lifted it. "Your eyes look clear," she said softly, and then turned to the door and screamed. "Her eyes are clear." I tried to talk, but Moulan put a finger to my lip. "Diva, Lagos, and Dexter are fine. They didn't nap as long as you did, lovely. Gingerbread snap?" she asked, shoving a plate of cookies in my face. I shook my head. I wasn't hungry.

"I'm ready to go to Shogun City," I said, barely able to get the sound out of my scratchy throat. Moulan pursed her lips.

"Well, aren't we ambitious this morning," she snapped, her lips tightened.

Delta walked in, his heavy boots echoed against the wood floor.

He and Moulan exchanged glances and she left.

"Sit beside me," I said to Delta. He obliged. I pushed myself up, leaned toward him and kissed him. It was as if I'd never kissed him before. And as our lips met, I could see the symbols in my mind. I reminded myself that this was my real world. This was the time and world that mattered, and yet I longed for a few more moments with Carcine Blackfoot. As soon as his name crossed my mind, Delta pulled away.

"I'll be outside," he yammered and left.

My legs felt wobbly, but I made myself walk around Moulan's palace. I needed the exercise. This return felt more loaded than the first. My body felt like a ton of achy bricks. I headed for the kitchen and passed an open door. A petite woman, her tightly curled black hair was a halo around her head. She shook her head quickly, as if shaking off a shiver and acknowledged me without turning around. "Come in," said Diva. I walked in.

"I had a daughter about your age," Diva said. "Moulan said she was snatched up by the Dirk," she said, her voice breaking. "And Illmatic, too." Diva wiped the tears from her eyes. I felt that I should comfort her, but I didn't know what to do. I'd been so self-absorbed. I hadn't thought about the Missing and their families or their readjustment to this life. "You're Illmatic's daughter," she said, half asking, half knowing.

"Yes," I said, inching toward her, but she pulled away from the window and over to a small chair and ornate table with a golden-framed mirror on the wall. She took a seat and looked at me through the mirror, nodding for me to sit as well. I perched on the edge of her narrow bed. She swiveled around to face me.

"Illmatic suspected this would never work. We screwed things up royally."

I was surprised that she felt responsible.

"It's not your fault," I added.

She gave me a quick lookover. I felt naked. We shared a love for my father, our planet, but it felt like there was an ocean of unsaid truths between us. We were from the same planet but from very different worlds. She once knew peace. I did not.

"You look like him," she added.

"Am I like him?" I asked. I was a little girl lost, yearning for a connection to a man I barely remembered.

"No," she said, snapping me back into the present.

"The life we made for our children was supposed to be better than this. We have to get back to earth," she added.

"But our flying machines don't work in this atmosphere, and we can't teleport because—"

"Hogwash," she added. "Shogun City has everything we need."

"You mean, we can get back to Earth," I asked?

"Of course," she said. "We just have to leave from Shogun City. That's where the energy threads are."

"Energy threads?" I repeated. It was the first time I'd ever heard of such a thing.

"It's a superhighway that takes you to Earth and back in seconds," said Diva.

"Does Moulan know about them?" I asked.

"She discovered them," Diva replied.

"Wait a minute," I said. "Then why didn't we go back there years ago to get help?"

"I don't know, Rayla. This world isn't like the one I left." Diva came close and peered into my eyes. "Go to Shogun City, find out what's happening and report back to me. Do not mention this conversation to anyone else," she added. "We don't know who we're dealing with. I need to know who is real and who is not."

"What about Moulan," I asked.

"She's the least of your worries, Illmatic," she said. Why was everyone so protective of Moulan?

"What about Rita?" I asked, I thought of telling Diva about the book, but she interrupted me."

"Please," she snapped.

"What about Delta?" I asked. Surely, she thought Delta could be trusted.

"The fact that you have to ask is an issue unto itself," she snipped. "I thought you were the daughter of Illmatic, the great neo astronaut. Never doubt your decisions. And never trust a son of Shogun," she added. "They look out for self above all else. We are at war. Haven't you figured that out yet?" I was well aware of the war, just not so clear on the enemy. I told Diva about the Disappearing Tigers and Sebastian's Caves. She listened.

"What are you thinking?" I asked, not able to read her.

"First things first," she said. With that, Diva went into the adjacent bedroom and slammed the door

Chapter 25

Singing Symbols

THE red sun hung high in the sky. Moulan's troops were hanging out as usual, watching the day turn to night, and drowning themselves in heapings of red soup and purple water, as Delta spun long tales of adventures long gone. I watched them laugh, smiling to myself that there's always joy in the most precarious of situations. Diva's charge intrigued me; and while I understood her reasons for secrecy, I didn't know how or if it played a role in the task before me. These strings she mentioned had me curious, as did this notion that getting to earth was a nonissue. Why hadn't I heard of these threads before? If we could get to earth and return, we could somehow end this war, or at least that's what I believed when I began. But with the recovery of some of the Missing, the revelation of Sui Lee's existence, and the looming underworld, not to mention this missing life of mine in Shogun City, my focus was completely off. Even Carcine was a distant memory. I thought of Rita, the Dirk, machine doubles, and the web of thinly laced lies that sang truths. What was the Crystal Cove, and why was every life so preoccupied with it? Where was it exactly? Just a figment of my dreams? A remnant of collective consciousness? What else had Moulan screwed up, and what was she afraid of? Each new turn was its own winding road, and I was beginning to find solace in the unpredictability of it all. Diva was neither a friend nor a foe. While I appreciated her expertise, I didn't feel anymore indebted to her than I did to Moulan. But Diva was at least right about one thing, I needed to remember who I was. While a trip to Shogun City could lead us to Earth, it was most important that I discovered myself, all of me. The soldiers were doubling over with laughter now, and I sauntered over to join them.

"All lies," I said. Walking up to the crew, Delta chuckled. "Duty calls," he said, half-jokingly to the crew and joined me.

"Good evening, Princess. I'm at your beck and call," he said with a bow and his typical sarcasm.

We walked off; and just when we were beyond earshot of the crew, I turned to Delta. "I'm ready," I said. Delta stopped in his tracks and raised an eyebrow.

"Ready to go to Shogun City?"

"Ready to be with you."

"Really?" he said. "What's with the change of heart?"

"I'm tired of being protected from myself. I live for the present, but I need to know my past. Come to Shogun City with me. "

I sat on the grassy hill expecting that Delta would sit beside me, but he just looked to the setting sun.

"Read page 53-399 of your book, and it should about cover it."

"Cover what?"

"Anything you need to know for the trip."

"I already read my book," I said.

"Read it again," he sneered. "Your story changes a lot," he said.

"Delta, I'm serious."

"So am I," he said. Delta's attitude flickered with the wind.

"Will you at least go with me?" I yelled after him.

"But of course, Princess," he said wryly and headed back to the camp.

Maybe Diva was right. A son of Shogun can never be trusted ... or loved.

I pulled out my book and read page 33 on. There was nothing new. I reread the pages again, looking for clues, a mention of Shogun, but there was none, nothing I hadn't read before. I was reading by starlight now; and just when I was ready to curse Delta to the wind, I noticed a poem, one I didn't recall reading anyway.

"The white cat dances

The white cat prances

The white cat jumps over the moon.

Ride up the raindrops and down through the sea

The white cat wants water at noon."

A silly poem, I thought. But silliness has its place, and it was the only phrase I found that resonated with truth. I let the poem ruminate; but I must have fallen asleep, because the next thing I remember was a large, warm hand shaking my shoulder.

"Delta," I said.

"Rayla," a familiar voice responded. I turned around and was greeted by Lagos. He towered over me like a tree providing shade, and the strength of his voice compelled me to stand.

"No, please. I'd like to join you." Lagos sat beside me, folding his legs underneath himself. "I'll begin by thanking you," he said, his warm smile bellowing from his belly.

"Is it nice to be back?" I asked.

"Of course," he said with a smile. Lagos had an easy disposition, and he didn't wear the guilt that Diva blanketed herself in. I enjoyed his charm, and there was something in his smile that was completely disarming. I could tell him anything.

"The others caught me up on our world's state. Despite it all, there's nothing like the beauty of two rising moons. Fills me with hope" I looked off beyond the horizon as our two dueling moons rose with nightfall. "Back in the other world, you said you saw those symbols before."

"Symbols?" Lagos was referring to the Crystal Cove and the symbols in the communication device.

"I knew who you were when you walked into the bar. I know who you are now. A daughter of Illmatic is easy to spot."

"You knew I was arriving? How did you know?"

"Because I listen." he said. "Do you really think a well-trained neo astronaut couldn't get back to this world?"

"You disappeared on purpose?" I asked, looking around to see if anyone could hear.

"Let's just say someone or something was complicating our return. But everything happens for a reason. Follow the threads, Rayla. The threads of time are speaking to us. They don't speak to everyone, but they speak to you. The Neo Astronauts will restore the balance, but our work is not your work. What are your plans?" he asked.

"I'm going to Shogun City," I told him, I wanted to read him, get his thoughts on the matter, but he gave me nothing. I told him about my Lost Years, what I hoped to learn. I told him how we got to this state, fighting from the Enchanted Forests. Lagos listened patiently.

"Sometimes we go on journeys only to discover that we already knew what we were looking for."

"Are you saying I shouldn't go?" I asked.

"I'm saying you already know the answers to your questions, and you should give some more thought to those symbols in the Crystal Cove."

"So I should stay?" I asked.

"Why are you so unsure of yourself?" he asked.

I didn't know. I wasn't always like this. But now, I was questioning myself and looking for him to give me answers that only I could find.

"Surely, you must find all of this as bizarre as I do," I said.

"I travelled to another world, hoping to discover new wonders, but the greatest wonder was me. I didn't discover a new planet, I discovered myself," he said.

"Tell me about your friend," he said. "Carcine. Isn't he your friend, too?"

I was stunned by the question, but I trusted Lagos and told him everything, about meeting Carcine, about the rebels, about his disappearance. When I was done I waited for Lago's to say something profound, but he sat in silence.

"Well," I said.

"He's in your heart. He's never far," he quipped.

"It doesn't matter where he is because I've moved on," I said.

"Stay focused, young Illmatic. Your charge is yours and yours alone." Lagos stood and extended his hand to help me up.

"Will you be joining us for a game of cards with Moulan?" he asked.

"What are cards?" I asked. He smiled and his beckoning grin was a sign to follow along.

***

Lagos and I entered Moulan's. Diva, Dexter, Enuk , Anna, and Scotch sat hunched over a four-corner table with numbered squares in their hands. A bevy of crystals sat in the middle. Anna slammed a square on the table.

"I win again," she squealed and gathered the crystals to her corner.

"Where's Moulan," I whispered to Lagos.

"Where she needs to be," he said. I was in a room of legends, Titans even. My God, this war was going to end, and these people knew how to end it. I couldn't stop smiling.

"So Illmatic, I hear you're going to Shogun City," Enuk said, rubbing his belly as he rocked his chair on its hind legs.

"Us neos aren't too fond of the place," said Dexter. "And neither was your dad."

"He hated it," chimed Diva. "Said it was the worst of the old world. Can't imagine that's changed much."

"Who'd of thought, of all the things that did change on this planet, that that egalitarian hellhole would be preserved? Unbelievable," said Anna.

"When we take out the Dirk, we'll have it dismantled," said Diva, smacking hands with Scotch. "Just like we'll dismantle the mind surveillance."

"If there is one," added Anna, as she rose up from the table to refill her thimble.

"We've got to get the others and fast," said Scotch.

"After we get the lay of the land," said Lagos. "When Rayla returns from Shogun City, we'll begin. Not a move until then. Beside, you quacks need to get in shape."

"How long you plan on staying, Illmatic?" asked Dexter, crossing his legs as he chewed on a twig. "I'm ready for some action."

"Not long," said Diva. "She knows we don't have time for her dillydal-lying."

"And the Shogun boy?" asked Anna.

122

"We'll deal with him later," she said.

A clanking noise echoed from the hallway. Everyone paused; moments later Moulan emerged in soot.

"You really dirtied yourself up this time," said Diva, the others laughed.

"I am happy to see you," Moulan said meekly, but the others ignored her.

"Anna, Scotch, and Enuk, you can scout out Sebastian's Cave," said Diva. "The rest of us will crack the mind surveillance."

"Try to reboot some of these computers," said Dexter, who left and headed down another corridor.

"When that's done, Moulan will reprogram the doubles in case we need power to take down the Tigers. Anna, Scotch, and Enuk popped up and headed for the hallway to Sebastian's Cave. Moulan turned to float off.

"Moulan," Lagos said. She whirled about slowly, her face unreadable and sat at the table.

Lagos took an empty seat and joined them.

"You broke our code of ethics, Moulan. At no point were you to go against Planet Earth's natural law."

Moulan cut her eyes. "What exactly is natural law in a world where you can create anything? Humans weren't born with wings, and yet we can fly. Is that defying natural law? You didn't seem to have a problem with it when we expanded the human life cycle. No death? I don't see you crying about that one."

"Time is a natural law," said Lagos. "Hijacking the future goes beyond all rules, and everyone's sense of humanity. As does forcing free people underground and recreating doubles without their permission."

"I did it to protect them. To protect you, all of you."

"That is yet to be determined," said Lagos. Lagos lasered in on Moulan, who stood abruptly.

"No," she screamed. Lagos created a force field around Moulan. She banged on it, she screamed, but no sound could be heard. She looked to me, but I didn't know what to do.

"Until further notice," said Lagos, he shouted, "you are an enemy of the state to be tried in court when one is assembled."

Delta busted through the door. "What is this?"

Lagos lasered in on Delta, creating a force field around him, too. I tackled Lagos, and he fell to the floor. Delta pulled out his sword to strike.

"No," I screamed.

"Delta's coming with me to Shogun City. We need him," I said.

"That's not your decision," said Diva, as Lagos composed himself and stood.

"I am not fighting one authoritarian regime to bow to another one. You don't make my choices."

"Then go," Lagos said. I looked to Moulan, trapped behind the invisible wall. I could not rescue her. I shouldn't rescue her, but I could not fault her for everything. I felt her words. "Do not let them get into the Crystal Cove. Do not let them have access to the library."

I looked to Moulan one last time, but Delta pulled me away. Delta's troops had the place surrounded, but we cut through them and headed for his lair. I could see the giant tree in the distance. My marks from my meager attempts to ax it had disappeared.   A golden rope fell from above, and both he and I climbed up through the branches and slipped into his palace of white. "Do you have Rita's book?" he asked. I nodded. He took my hand, and we walked through a door into the dark maze that leads to Rita's and to Shogun. We ran through the familiar brick hallways, past the spot where the Tigers almost captured us and slipped down a shoot that took us to another level below. This one was laced with bricks of gold. We ran a bit further and stopped at a tall green door with heavy golden door knockers.

"I'm sorry that you have to find out this way," said Delta.

"It is what it is, Delta," I said.

I reached for the door knockers.

"Before you go inside, I want you to know that I love you."

"I love you, too," I said.

"Everything that I've done, I did because I loved you. My sarcasm just masks my pain."

Delta's outpouring made me feel uncomfortable.

"And I love Moulan," he said. "She's like a mother to me."

"I'm sorry about—"

"She's fine," he said. "Moulan will always be fine. But you—"

A jostling noise interrupted us. Someone was opening the door. I stepped back as it creaked open and was greeted by my own eyes. A woman in a soft blue gown and dark hair that flowed like water, a mirror image of myself stared back to me. My heart stopped.

"Finally," she said with a hearty smile.

"My other me has returned. And you brought your husband with you," she turned to someone behind her. "Honey, come look."

The spitting image of jollier Delta in a lush red robe appeared.

"How delightful," he bellowed. "Is it time for the switch already?"

"Well don't just stand there," the other me continued. "Come inside, both of you."

Delta took my hand, but my feet were planted into the ground. I couldn't move, my head was spinning, and my stomach flipped. Delta swung me into his arms. "Oh look, honey. He's carrying her over the threshold, like a new bride," the blue-haired double cooed. Delta carried me into their grand room. Through my dizziness, I could see that it was much brighter than Moulan's; but the décor, this ancient style of plush living, was the same. Delta gently placed me on a multipatterned couch, with colors so wild, my head spun more.

"She needs water," a familiar voice said. I heard the hills clicking first. Rita stood before me. She squatted down and handed me a glass of clear liquid.

"You won't find any like this on the rest of Planet Hope," she said. She snatched my bag and grabbed her book. I sipped the clear liquid.

"Thank you. You will be rewarded." She stood and turned to face the handful of people peppered throughout the room.

"The true king and queen have arrived. Arrest the imposters."

With that, two guards snatched up the woman in blue and the other Delta. The other Delta tried to fight back, but he was quickly succumbed. They threw black bags over their heads and ushered them out the room.

I'm a queen?

Logic escaped me, but I found myself talking as if I knew these people, this world.

"Do not execute them," I said. "We grant mercy to the merciful," I said. What was I doing?

The others in the room looked to one another and nodded.

"You are the wise one. The wisest of them all," said a large round-faced man with red cheeks and shoes that curled up. His fur cloak and beaded pants jostled as he walked. I felt that I was slipping into something else, into someone else.

"She needs a moment," said Delta. And the others scurried out.

I looked at the room of gold and silver. Everything in this place bounced off sunlight, as if someone spent a lifetime polishing it. Unlike Moulan's haunts that inked with oddities, this place felt perfect, too perfect. A painting of me in a big red-feathered gown hung on the wall before me. At the bottom it read, Queen Rayla Redfeather. Delta had a lot of explaining to do. But I couldn't digest anymore with this spinning head.

"Welcome home, Rayla," Delta said, placing a wet rag over my eyes and forehead.

I didn't respond. I needed sleep, but the thin line between dream and reality made the thought of resting a joke. I peeled the rag off my eyes and forehead.

"You have some explaining to do," I said.

"How should I begin?" he said.

"Start backwards. Moonwalk it in," I said. I walked over to one of the dozen windows that engulfed the room. Beyond these walls was a bustling city with all the feats of architecture past and present that one could imagine. The beauty was overwhelming.

"This is our city," Delta said, whispering in my ear as he wrapped his arms around me.

This is my city, I thought. I felt a surge of power overtake me. Yes, this was all mine, and this was all me.

"Do the Neo Astronauts know about me and this world?"

126

"Who are the Neo Astronauts," said Delta with a smile. And suddenly, I didn't care much about them either with their lost planet and truth-fueled ways. Shogun City is my home.

"I like it here," I said.

"Of course you do. I'll explain everything, but for now just enjoy. I'll protect you. The Shangos will protect you."

"I can protect myself," I said, but I was thirsty. That clear liquid was the best I'd ever had.

Delta poured another glass for me.

"Drink up."

I guzzled it down, and Delta kissed some of the liquid off my neck.

"Which me is the real me?" I asked, trying to grip onto some reality as I felt the weight of worry slip away.

"In the morning I'll tell you everything," he said.

But the days were so pretty here, I wondered if they even had nightfall. Delta took a large black disc and placed it on some square object. He lifted a lever and placed it on one of the grooves in the disc. I could hear the words and sounds of the old world philosopher Stevie Wonder. Wonder's syrupy voice was hypnotizing. He said something about early May. May sound like such a lovely place. May, what's May? I wondered. I tried to ask Delta, but he spun me around and pinned me to his chest. We danced like there was no tomorrow, we danced with all the fervor of two people who needed release and craved the love of rhythm. We danced into what would be nightfall; except in Shogun City, the sun never set. Ever.

***

Chants and yells engulfed Moulin's Palace, but the troops of human doubles she summoned couldn't get through the door. Lagos' force field was a steel wall, and the lasers the troops were firing couldn't penetrate. "How long can you hold them off," asked Diva, as she and Lagos flipped through Moulan's library of books? The library stretched for miles, but Diva and Lagos were making ground.

"As long as we need to," said Lagos. "We're not going to find it in here."

Dexter ran into the library exasperated, beads of sweat pouring from his temples. "There's no trace of the Dirk anywhere, and I can't detect a mind-

127

tracking system either."

"Are you sure about that?" said Lagos.

"Positive. But uh, I also don't detect anything else either, sir."

"What do you mean?" he asked.

"I'm not getting a signal for human life. None in the Enchanted Forest and definitely none in the cities, except Shogun City."

Lagos and Diva looked to one another.

"But that's not all. I did some planet assessments and our coordinates are off."

"The planet rotation has changed?"

A bead of sweat ran from Dexter's temple into his eyes. He wiped it away.

"I uh, don't think we're on Planet Hope."

"Then where are we?"

"I don't know, sir."

Lagos stormed out the library to Moulan's force field prison.

But she was gone. When he turned back to the library, Dexter and Diva had escaped just in time before the library vanished.

"To Sebastian's Cave," he yelled. And all three ran to the long hallway, flipped back the metal lid, and climbed down the hole. Diva and Dexter jumped in first. Lagos was sure to close the lid tightly behind him.

As he flew down the rabbit hole, he thought of Rayla and her treks in Shogun City. If she didn't return soon, he would simply have to find her. This lost daughter was the only walking memory of his good friend Kent, and he felt indebted to maintaining her well-being, even if she was uncharacteristically confused, something he attributed to whatever happened during her lost years and Sui Lee's overprotectedness. He just was not up for another war with the Shangos. Planet Hope did not believe in war. Then he reminded himself that this virtual playground they were climbing through might not be Planet Hope after all, making a Shango battle in Shogun City justified. He smiled. It was the only happy thought he'd had since he returned.

RAYLA'S
REVOLUTION

3

Chapter 26

Woman in the Mirror

Is this an interrogation room? The four white walls and the hollow silence indicate that others were around. I sat at a wooden table in a tiny chair with uneven legs. An infinite mirror that stretched the width of the room was placed in front of me. Perhaps the hidden others were behind it. My smiling face was a bit too jovial for the moment and that's when I realized there was no mirror before me, but rather a warm and fuzzy duplicate of myself. She wore a white top with thin straps. I wore the same top in Mayan blue.

"Good Day, Rayla," it said, with the sunny ring of one who relished in happy times.

"Who are you?" I asked. She peered left and right, as if others were listening and leaned in with a smile.

"Well, I'm not you," she said.

"No, kidding," I snapped.

"Look, we don't have time for a full data swap. Per your instructions, if danger is near, I am to shut down and lock all files of your memory until all is clear. And danger is near. But you programmed this briefing to minimize all confusion. Are you confused?"

"Yes," I said.

"You predicted that. So, per your instructions you are to be reminded of your mission," she said.

"To go to Earth," I said.

"Why yes, you remembered," she said with a grin.

"And don't let anyone into the Crystal Cove," I said.

"You are amazing," she said. "Why you don't need me at all."

"I'm ready for the full data swap," I said.

"I cannot do that," she said.

"Yes, you can," I repeated. "There is no danger pending."

"Access denied," she said. "Access denied. Access denied." Her voice grew angrier with each repetition as her smile hardened and nearly cracked. I stood, it stood, and then someone blindsided me and tackled me to the ground.

***

Sunlight cascaded into my bedroom through the open balcony, tickling my face and coercing an awakening. I'm residing in the silence of morning, this fresh day that feels like night. The sun is so bright. Was the sun always this brilliant? The sheets are so soft, almost too soft, like I am a pea nestled in a hefty bed of feathers. The bed hugged me, massaged me. I didn't want to leave its snug embrace, but those tickling sunrays wouldn't allow another lazy hour or three.

Delta stood radiant on the balcony, overlooking the busy city we shared with the grace of a demigod from yesteryear. His silk blue pants fluttered with the light breeze, and the light danced on his bronzed chest. He was a man who had a natural pose, too, one captured by a master artist who chiseled his likeness into a statue that stood at the center of town. Shoulders back, chest lifted, leaning back on the right leg with his left mounted at the foot of the gold rail, Delta was unforgettable. I enjoyed looking at him. For a flash, I felt as if this was my first time truly seeing him. Nonsense.

I am awake. I found myself reminding me of that, repeating it in my head over and over, hoping to pull myself away from the lull of the dream. But I couldn't shake off the shrieking nightmare, a reccurring dream, a tug of war with me fighting in dreary caves and creepy dungeons. There was a green-eyed witch, an angry astronaut, and a ragged and weary with an impenetrable drive that zipped me from one battle to the next. And that angry robot screaming. I thought of recording the whole saga in our digital files while I still remembered it; but Delta noticed I was awake, breaking from his statuesque stance and joined me.

"Good morning, Rayla," he said, easing onto the edge of the bed beside me. He kissed me lightly on the forehead. A butterfly kiss. "How do you feel?"

he asked.

"Awake," I said.

"Hmmm," he said, inspecting my face with his gaze.

"And I had the craziest dream," I said.

"Aren't they all?" he added.

I recounted some of the horrors of me running and fighting and search-
ing for God knows what. "Then there was a couple that looked just like you and
I," I said. "Droids or clones. Plain awful. The whole thing was exhausting," I said.
"Who can rest with dreams like that?"

"So why don't you?" he asked.

"Because we have work to do," I said.

He brushed my curled hair back from my face. His soft lips pressing
against my forehead again. "Doesn't feel like you have a fever today. So I guess
that dream of yours was real."

"Jokes," I retorted, sinking into the sheets. This bed was so comfortable,
like I hadn't slept in it in years; and yet I felt as if all I'd done was sleep. Nonsense.

"No, really, Rayla," he said with all the earnestness he could muster. "It
really happened."

I cut my eyes and rolled over, nestling my head back into the deeply
set feather-stuffed pillows. He kissed my shoulder and dangled a snake-twisted
locket with a blue stone in my face. I shot up, the reality hitting me like a flying
asteroid to the dome. "We have to, we have to," I didn't know what to say. My
heart raced to the beat of the spinning room. Delta rubbed my arm and stopped
the rotation.

"We have to relax," he said. "When you're ready, we'll have lunch with
the Delights. They're waiting for you."

I raced through the files in my mind, sifting through to recall my focus.
The Neo Astronauts want me to survey the scene, Moulan wants to keep the
library out of the hands of the astronauts, Rita has her book, and Sui Lee wants
to protect the people in the cave. I thought of the strings, going back to Earth and
Carcine. Oh, my Carcine. How long had I forgotten about him? But what do I want
in this mess of a moment?

I thought of Diva's warning. My recollection of the Lost Years was surfacing slowly. The items in the bedroom were ones I'd seen before, all old-world items: palm sized crystal birds, glass bowls of rubies and diamonds, and a red-feathered fan that spanned the wall. The rest of the room was spruced with tapestries in rich blue, and I was reminded of my astral travel to East Africa. But this wasn't East Africa. These were my belongings, but this room was not mine. The strings. I need to get to Earth.

"We're not in our palace," I said.

"No, we aren't," Delta replied. "We're here at the pleasure of the Delights. They are downstairs when you're ready." Delta's regal baring was a substitute for his usual wisecracks, and this switch in demeanor felt as foreign as this faintly familiar room. Streams of memories were flooding my mind. Flashing images of an intense fight of some sort, an escape, a caged fortress.

I slipped out of the covers and circled the room. I looked out over the balcony. In the distance just beyond the field of green grass lay the heart of Shogun City, the towering crystal skyscrapers glistened in the morning sun. In fact, I spotted a palace. The gold dome shimmered in the sea of crystal, but all I could remember were the wide hallways and their ornate rugs. I surveyed the land bringing my eyes to the ground just below. Two men and one woman, armed in elaborate red armor with padded shoulders stood below me. My predicament was obvious. "We're in prison," I said.

What did I do? I wondered. I flipped through images, rapid-fire frames of life paired with old ones and other times. I led a fight, a battle, but for what? I was captured, but somehow I slipped away, back to the Enchanted Forest. Who was I fighting?

Delta snuggled up behind me and wrapped his arms around my waist. "It will all make sense in a moment," Delta said, kissing my cheek. "Edna and Jaggi are downstairs. They took great pains to see you." But I wasn't ready to see the Delights yet, still mulling over my whereabouts.

"We're enemies of the state," I said, in a half whisper so soft; I wondered if Delta heard me."

"That's one way of looking at it," he said. "Not everyone overtakes the Shangos, dethrones the aristocracy and lives to tell about it."

"I overthrew the aristocracy?"

"No, we overthrew the aristocracy. Amazing feat. And for a year or so we ran things smoothly. But we were captured. Didn't last long, though."

"The doubles," I said.

"Pretty good likeness, if I do say so myself. Awesome decoy for a great escape," he added with the cavalier attitude. "And now you've returned. When you decide what you want done with them, we'll have them dismantled."

"Dismantled?" I shouted. I pulled away and grabbed my book from my raggedy satchel, and the book was open to the page of my present. Rayla's Return. Those were the only words scribbled on the page.

A knock at the door tossed me out of my confusion. Delta went to the door, cracking it just enough for me to see nothing.

"She's not ready, yet," he said and shut the door.

"Who was that?" I asked.

"A lot of people have been waiting for your return. So when you're ready."

"Ready for what?" I asked.

"Ready to claim your future. There are people who will help you."

Does claiming my future mean saving Planet Hope? I thought of the Neo Astronauts and their wishes. How can I claim a future when I barely know my past; when I'm wrestling with the present; when I'm wrestling with who I am? But memories were resurfacing, like those slice frames of images I saw with Carcine, where all that was light was dark and the reverse. I could see fragments of things from the past that I had to decipher.

Frames of red fluttered my memory. Fights with the Shangos. Victory. But the high was a low. "So I led a revolution, I fought the Shangos, tried to topple the leadership, and was imprisoned, then created doubles of ourselves to escape to Planet Hope?" I looked to Delta for confirmation but he said nothing. It didn't make any sense.

"Why weren't we killed?" I asked. Why would the Shogun City rulers allow us to live?

"Because you are loved." My mind projected images of happy crowds. I didn't believe him. I wanted to remember so badly I could taste the residue of the lost past in my mouth. Why was Delta so hyped for us to return to a prison? How was I supposed to find my future in a well-decorated prison?

I patted my hand along the cold stone walls, feeling for the warmth of the tunnel that leads us here. Delta stretched out on the bed and watched. I almost ran my hand across a gold panel, but he bolted up.

135

"Don't touch that," he said. "One swipe and you'll retrigger the brain monitors. Way back in yesteryear when you were plotting our escape, you created a system to block the mind surveillance in this room. You were tired of shielding yourself with your own powers, so you had this bedroom rewired. Brilliant," he said. "While you recalibrated the mind reading scans, you couldn't block the body movement sensors, and that's how the doubles were born."

I sidestepped the gold panel and continued feeling about. Was the door that I reentered gone?

"You'll never find it," he said.

"Then help me," I demanded.

"Can't," he said. "You blocked it when you arrived, so that you wouldn't run away. And you're blocking my ability to find it, too. I guess you feared this moment would come."

"Why didn't you stop me?" I shouted.

"It's hard to stop a determined woman," he said. I raced back to the balcony and looked down below. I could take out troops below. But the Originals and the Shangos would tail me. No locks, no chains. There must be more sensor barricades that I can't see.

"It is time to face your future, Rayla Illmatic."

I didn't want to face anything until my memory was fully restored. These flashes of images just weren't enough to go on. I circled about took a deep breath and stopped. I would make this moment mine. But things weren't adding up.

"Access denied," I mumbled. What was I saying?

I took a seat on a soft red chair, grabbed my book, and opened to a random page. It was blank. Blank like my mind, blank like my memory.

I took a few deep breaths. Placing my hand on my chest, I caressed the pendant on my necklace. Stop thinking and be, I said to myself. The tightness in my shoulders eased some. I thought of the Crystal Cove and the abounding peace. I thought of Vietnam. I thought of DC. I thought of the wedding that never was. I thought of Carcine. Lost in time. Lost to me. I thought of my father. I thought of Notia, my lost friend in Africa.

But when flashes of a Shogun City surfaced, all I could remember was a swath of anger, a rash of calculated actions, a fight, containment, an escape. The players in this saga and the why behind the game were puzzle pieces. My travels through time had made me acclimated to this state. I reminded myself that this intensity of the moment, one with a blurred past, was a state I'd grown accustomed to. Today was no different and I relaxed.

I exhaled. But all was not right.

"Delta, it sounds to me like I was a pretty savvy lady during my Shogun years."

"I would agree," he said. "And you still are. You really should give yourself more credit, Rayla. You always underestimate yourself."

"I had it all covered, even my escape," I said.

"You're a strategist," he said. "The best."

Sui Lee was better, I thought. But Planet Hope wasn't designed for war and this military mind-set was about getting us back on track only. I didn't know how the skills applied in peace. The only peace I knew were those moments in the Crystal Cove. But strategizing does sharpen mental acumen. I had an ability to sift past the haziness of a larger picture and laser in on the essential point. Maybe this was the gift Rita spoke of. I was not easily distracted, and once I found a line of inquiry to pursue, a nugget of truth, I drilled down on it like a miner on a quest for precious stones. And of all the nonsensical happenstance of a fuzzy past that landed me in a prison, there was one point that made the least sense of them all.

"How did I lose my memory? That, I can assure you, I did not do myself," I quipped.

"How did you lose your memory," Delta repeated. He cleared his throat. "The first time or the second time?"

"How many times did I lose it?" I asked. He motioned to answer, but I stopped him. I could only take in so much, and I was veering on overload. I returned to the finer point.

"The one that landed me with Carcine and the rebels," I said. The mention of Carcine's name made Delta stiffen. His cavalier cool slipped into mild anxiety. He cracked a knuckle, and the door bolted open. I could hear the voice, but I couldn't see the face. "The Delights are waiting."

Chapter 27

Deep Sea Flying

"They want to be discovered, but they have to discover themselves"

— Anonymous via Skype, Earth Summer, 2013

ACCORDING to Delta, Rita had alerted Edna and Jaggi that I'd returned. For 75 years, they amused a flesh-and-bone double during their visits, acting with all the theatrics they could muster to keep the Shangos at bay. I had to be as still as possible, mimicking the double I'd created, so that I did not cause any suspicion among the sensors. My arrest had taken a great toll in the Delights and their social standing' and they were virtually Outkasts in a city where they were once beloved, Delta said. Edna was a petite, gentle woman, whose syrupy voice was made for soothing souls. A singer, she still on occasion performed, although her ranking as singer of the nation had slipped significantly since my arrest, Delta said. Her brown mossy hair was wound into a bun; and for the day, she wore a pink kimono with dyed green ivy etched in spider silk.

But her sunken eyes, worn with years of worry, carried a sparkle today. Jaggi, a jolly fellow, as he described himself, a man with a slight build and round belly said today was his St. Nick day, and he adorned the red suit of the fabled Santa Claus. His black hair was slicked back into a ponytail that fell below the fur in his cap. These were the people who raised me, the ones who Rita and Sui Lee entrusted me to. The four of us sat around a wooden table in our entertaining room, one of the handfuls of luxuries we were permitted to live with in our exile.

Our prison itself was far from the worst. We lived in a modest cottage with two floors, a parlor, small kitchen and dining room on the first, with our bedroom and restroom on the second. We had no access to the world database, not even an old digitablet, and absolutely no books. The accommodations, which were far from meager, were considered punishing by Shogun standards. But looking at the Jaggis, some details did surface. Delta and I had caused an uproar that split the city's populace in two, with some in our corner and others pleading for our demise. Edna and Jaggi were among those who pleaded for mercy; and the council of elders, the wise rulers of Shogun City, voted for exile over death. The Shangos, who were once like family to me, were now duty-bound to prevent our escape. Jaggi, who had once served on the council himself, requested that we stay in their summer home beyond the city. The elders agreed.

The memories were coming fast now. This prison was once a place where I, along with the Jaggis, would retreat during the season change to live "the simple life." We made old-world jams, rode horses, and took long walks in the orchards beyond the cottage gate. But as a child, while playing a game of hide and seek, I stumbled on yet another door to the Originals' maze, just beyond the closet in the upper bedroom. This door later became my escape route and my reentry. How the door got there is beyond me; but the cottage was an old one, a remnant from the Shogun City founders that Jaggi inherited from an uncle before he moved to the other world.

I have to find that door.

Delta and I ate a lunch that Delta had prepared: cold meat sandwiches on bread with yellow paste. Apparently, as part of our punishment, we had to make our own food, which was delivered to us by a prison assistant once a week. The Delights couldn't stop talking. They munched and talked as if the two motions were one. Delta, at some point, left the room for us to be alone. But I had a hard time connecting with the Delights. They talked and talked to the point of bewilderment about anything and everything but the happenings in Shogun City. Their banter rang like riddles.

"Her cheeks aren't very rosy," Edna said, giving me a mother's lookover. "A hint of rouge should do some good."

"But if she smiles brightly, no one will care about red cheeks, Edna," said Jaggi.

"What if we bought her a cat?"

"A white one," said Jaggi. "Well, only if it can jump over the moon."

They were in total denial of my predicament and rattled off color quips as if they were the most logical insights in the lexicon. I was still connecting dots about my past and whereabouts, but the Delight's chatter wasn't helping.

"So what's new?" I asked, prodding them along to talk about the current state of affairs.

"Nothing," said Jaggi, munching on his sandwich and dusting the crumbs away.

"There's nothing new under the sun," said Edna. "And with that cat not jumping over the moon."

"There will always be old things under the sun," continued Jaggi. "Really, who ever heard of something new under the sun?" he asked.

As they babbled relentlessly, it dawned on me that this mindless chatter was what Sui Lee prayed I would avoid. But their insistence on it intrigued me, and I soon realized that this was a strategy at which point Jaggi slipped his hand into an inner pocket near his chest and removed a small vial with a rolled-up document inside. Edna put her fingers to her lips, urging me not to comment. I smiled, and the two returned my gesture with a nod. I slipped the vial in my pocket. A Shango guard swung the door open. Our time together was over. Delta hadn't returned to say goodbye, and the Shango guard didn't wait for him.

"Well you have a grand day," Edna replied. Jaggi pulled the chair from under her as she stood.

"Yes, have a great one," he repeated. I hugged them both, squeezing tightly before the two exited swiftly. The bells on Jaggi's boots rang with each step. But the lone Shango guard remained. His name was Dayo Rodriguez. All the memories hadn't returned, but he was a friend. After Dayo was done with his search, he closed the curtains on the two small windows in the parlor.

"Time for the weekly sweep," he said dryly, before removing a scanner and waving it around every item in the house. He performed a thorough search, looking through cookie jars, drawers, under seat cushions. And when he was done he swept the top bedrooms, too. Finally, he returned.

"Welcome home, Rayla," Dayo said. "The brain sensors on this floor are disabled temporarily. We only have a few moments to speak freely."

I remembered Dayo more clearly now; he, too, was trained alongside me and Delta, during the Shogun training. He was more of a scientist than a warrior, but his knowledge of the sciences were beyond most. I stood to hug Dayo, my trusted friend. He was truly surprised and hugged me back with some reluctance. I then remembered my reentry into Shogun City. Dayo stood in the background; and when I demanded that the lives of the doubles be spared, it was he who bagged their heads and marched them off. If I was just a prisoner, why did they even listen to my commands, I wondered. Playing into my delusions, I assume, or were they afraid?

"Where are the doubles?" I asked Dayo. "They are in greenhouse, not too far from here," he said. A haunting flash captured my imagination. I saw Dayo and I inserted a needle into a body. I shook the image off. Did we create them together? I wondered.

"How did we make them?" I asked. Dayo was uneasy, he glanced toward the stairway leading up to my bedroom and back to me. He looked at his watch.

"You created them, Rayla, not me." I couldn't swallow the fact that I had made my own double. My stomach flipped just thinking about it. But maybe the extreme circumstance led to an even more extreme matter and I had no choice, just like Moulan had no choice. Both of us creating doubles for our own protection. How odd?

"I created them to live as Delta and I, while I escaped to the Enchanted Forest?" I asked.

"Rayla, you did a lot of things that were hard to explain,"he said flatly. "You only have ten seconds left to speak freely before the tracker comes back on."

"I need to get to Earth," I said. "I've found some of the Neo Astronauts, I've travelled to other dimensions. I need the strings." Dayo cut me off.

"I'm glad that you're back," said Dayo quickly, slipping out the door.

I pulled the curtain back and watched Dayo chat with the other guards before taking his post a meter or so in front of the door. What did Dayo mean when he said that I did many things that he didn't understand? I pulled out the vial that the Delights sent me, removed the tiny document, and unrolled it. "The crown is still yours for the taking," it read. I placed the scroll in my pocket and pulled on the cottage door. It was unlocked. How odd. I could see the top of a small greenhouse on a hill in the near distance. The holding point for the doubles, no doubt. Could I travel to the greenhouse and back without anyone seeing me? Could I take the skills Moulan taught me and travel short distances instantly in real time? I closed my eyes and burned the image of the greenhouse in my mind. The greenhouse image dissipated into the Crystal Cove. After bathing in the glow of the crystals I opened my eyes.

I did it. The greenhouse was stocked with exotic plants. Flowers in full bloom leaned toward the flood of sunlight. A bevy of leafy plants formed an arch over the center of the greenhouse. That's where the double Delta and me sat at a table sipping tea.

"Ah, you've arrived," the other me said. She still adorned her blue gown and ran up to hug me tightly. I wanted to pull away but chose not, too.

"Come," she said, beckoning me to sit with them. I obliged.

"What should I call you?" I asked.

"Call me U," she said with a smile.

"You?" I asked.

"No, U as in the letter U. Rhymes with hue. Not Y.O.U."

"Good for clarity," said the other Delta.

"Tea?" she asked, reminding me of Moulan's formalities. U stretched across the table and poured the steaming liquid from a round pot into a palm-sized cup. She resembled me, but her happy-go-lucky demeanor and erudite flairs were all her. I would never be this prim and demure. Her hair was coiled into a basket of tiny braids. She adorned a mole on her cheek. I did not. And her smile, while pleasant, was mechanical. The marvel of science. You can copy yourself and still I stand apart.

"No, thank you," I said to the tea inquiry. "I just have a few questions."

"Of course. Are you sure you don't want any?"

"Yes," I said.

"And what else are you sure of?" said the other Delta, sitting back straight, chest poked in his chair.

"That's why I'm here. I'm not quite sure what I'm sure of anymore."

"You created us," said U. "We can't outsmart our maker."

"Not that we would want to," said the other Delta.

"The Shangos, for one are very upset with you. You betrayed them. You were to uphold their values and the values of Shogun City, above all else. But you overtook them, went against the ruling Council Elders, and seized the throne. You ruled for a spell, but there were so many forces working against you that they were able to capture you. It is because of the people and the people only that you and we are alive today. As a foreigner, you weren't trusted, anyway. The Shangos and the Council Elders were convinced that by allowing you in, that they'd made a mistake."

"A grave mistake," said the other Delta. "And they were correct."

"Why did I want to rule?" I asked.

"Because you could," said U. "If anyone were to upset the apple cart, it would be you. You were a prized pupil."

"Just you being U," said Delta with a smile.

Why would I do that, I wondered? "Perhaps I wanted to open the doors of the city," I said.

The two looked at one another and shook their heads.

"Not that we know of," said U.

"You broke every rule of the Shogun Order," added the other Delta. "You broke nearly every rule of the City."

"You made yourself and us queens in a Democracy," said U.

"For the progress of the people?" I asked.

"No, because you could," said U. "You, we are a bit rambunctious and thirsty. Are you sure you don't want any tea?"

"Perhaps it was teen rebellion," said U. "You were a tad angry about your lot. The Shangos sought to give you discipline."

"So much for that," chimed Delta.

I didn't want to believe them. I would not upset the order of things just for the sake of doing so. Clearly, I was trying to free the people. I had a goal, a mission.

"Are they angry with Delta?" I asked.

The two shook their heads in unison.

"Not so much," they said with the timber of a choir. This life to die for that Rita mentioned with glee seemed to have done nothing but wreak havoc; but it was all for a reason, I'm sure. I asked the twosome about the strings to Earth, but they claimed that they had no information on it.

"Now that you've returned, what will you do with us?" asked U.

"I don't' know," I said. "What do you suggest?"

"Keep us around," she said. "We do come in handy. Although our very existence is against the law. Planet Hope and Shogun City banned cloning many years ago," U said.

"But rules mean very little to you anyway," said the other Delta.

"Thank you," I said.

"No, thank you," they responded in unison.

I closed my eyes, slipped into the Crystal Cove and awakened standing on the main floor of the cottage. The guards didn't appear to notice anything. Dayo turned around, caught my eye and winked without the others noticing.

I could travel in real time, teleport in the blink of an eye from one distance to the next, from one time to another, just like my father could. Did Moulan simply mold a talent I already had? I didn't want to trigger the Shango's mind surveillance, so I headed to the second floor.

I marched up the creaky stairway to the bedroom and shut the door. I didn't know what to make of this power-thirsty me that U spoke of. She certainly wasn't the me that I knew. And I was also mulling over this talent I had, one that Delta must share, too. How do I use this gift and this knowledge to press forward to Earth? "We need to find the strings and get to Earth," I said. "Do you know where they are?" I asked. Do I even need them, I wondered. Delta was quiet. I thought of Diva's warning. "Never trust a son of Shogun City."

"Delta, this city must have ships that we can use to get back to Earth. They either have ships or these mythical strings. You were born and raised here, so tell me, which one is it?"

Delta didn't respond right away; and rather than wait for his answer, I headed back to the balcony, looking as the clouds sailed across the blue sky. I let the silence float like a cloud between us. I didn't fear his answer, I feared my response. Where was my spaceship, I wondered? Where was my sailing ark? Did Rayla Redfeather know how to travel in real time? My Lost Years were no accident. Delta spun me around to face him.

"I wiped your memory, Rayla. It was for your protection," he said. "I had to protect us and I had to protect you."

"From what?" I asked, the fever of the words rattled me to the core. He peered deeply into my eyes, so deeply that I could feel his gaze imprinted on my soul. "From yourself," he said.

144

I stepped back in shock. With each step I took back, Delta took another forward.

"That wasn't your decision, Delta."

He wiped my memory the night of our escape from Shogun City's prison, while I was sleeping in the maze, and dumped me into the world of the rebels, he said. "You weren't using your power rationally, and I feared that you'd become unstoppable. Your energy was too high. The Shangos would figure out that the prisoners were doubles, they would hunt you down and kill you. You needed to lie low, but that way of thinking was not in your vocabulary."

"You took away my power," I said.

"You were on a warpath that would have run us all off the cliff," he said. "I had to stop you."

"No one stops me," I said.

"I stopped you," he said. "You have no idea who you'd become. They would have picked up on your radar, and they would have found you. But I knew you could be saved. I loved you."

Delta went on to find Moulan, protecting her while she sorted out this mess. He formed an army and he waited. When the time was right, we would be one, he said. That time was now.

"I apologize," he said, throwing his hands around me and burying his face into my neck. Delta's tears ran down my shoulders. He cried so hard, I struggled to hold him up.

Why didn't he take me with him? Why leave me in a war zone with no memory? Why leave me vulnerable and open to attack? How was there any safety in abandonment? I would never do that to him, I thought. But the truth of the matter was I didn't know what I'd do. This Rayla Redfeather, Shango warrior who conquered Shogun City, was a stranger, a ghost. She was no more me than I was the clone I created.

For some unexplained reason, I empathized with Delta. Knowing that the woman he loved was completely unaware of their time together must have split his heart in two. And for a moment, I was saddened by my inability to recognize our shared bond, to feel a love that should have transcended the thin veil of time and memory in the Enchanted Forest we met again. But I was angry, too. The fury that teetered like a volcano was only contained by love, a true love. Love was our bond where memories weren't. Why would he need to protect me from myself? I wondered why couldn't I have the power of my own memory? Who was he to decide what was best for me?

"That wasn't your decision to make," I told him.

"I had no choice. You'd gone too far," he said.

"How far?" I asked. But Delta was buried in sobs.

Knowing that Delta was somehow responsible for this lapse helped me regain my composure. There was a security in at least knowing and there was a weird comfort in knowing that it was love that led Delta to make this bizarre decision and embark on this lucid quest. He was so heartbroken over this actions, and I reminded myself that I would address this later. I had gone too far. How is that possible? For now, I held him, stroking his tense back and face and reminding him that all was well. I would have to plot my escape from this prison he was so eager to get me back to, a four walled fortress that forced me to acknowledge a past love for him and a me I didn't know.

No explanation by Delta, the Delights, or the Shangos would justify this trickery they called life. Nor did I need any miscalculated self-indulgent protection from myself. "It will all make sense. I promise," he said between the rivers of tears. Maybe he was right. I would bide my time in this weirdness, gathering enough intelligence to end this war and go home. But a tear ran down my face, anyway. I began sobbing, realizing that home for me was as elusive as the Crystal Cove. Home could very well be a myth, too. Was I, too, a walking myth?

"We have to break out of here," I reminded him. But in between the tears, I feared that he would be content to stay in love with me behind this gated fortress forever. Yes, we needed to escape.

Chapter 28

Arguments in Color

DELTA and I fell asleep in one another's arms when a blaring static noise pierced our ears. Delta rose up from the bed and grabbed a small ancient metal device that he held to his ear.

"Silverado Diego is on his way," he said. "It's a scrambler," he said, pointing to the device. Picks up conversations around the perimeter. Dayo gave it to me."

"If you were a real Shango, you wouldn't need that thing," I said.

"Everyone's not an intuit," he chimed. "And those who are, don't always know how to use it," he quipped. "As you now know." Another dig into the unmemorable past. Delta, it seemed, had recovered from his bout of sadness. His sarcasm was in full swing.

Silverado Diego, I had no memories of him. I asked Delta for details.

"Silverado Diego is head of the Shangos, Rayla. He was our trainer. He was the one you overthrew. He's the reason we're in exile."

"Maybe I should just apologize to him and end this," I said.

"Unfortunately, it's not that simple. Just listen to him," Delta said. "Don't commit to anything. Don't reveal too much. Protect yourself. You chose to come here for a reason."

I heard a commotion outside. Three men in red hovercrafts pulled up.

147

The tallest of the three stepped off his ship. I opened my bedroom door and was greeted by Dayo.

"You have a guest downstairs," he said. I nodded and followed him. Delta was behind me.

"Just her," said Dayo. Delta obliged and reentered the bedroom.

Silverado Diego had made himself at home in the parlor. He drank a steaming liquid from a cup, wiped his mouth, and leaned back in the wood chair on one leg before crashing all four to the ground. A tall man with a barrel chest, he sported a sleek white beard of curls, a contrast to his bald head and dark eyes. His long blood-red cloak swung like one of Moulan's dresses and dark, heavy boots, ramming his high pointy heel into the floor with every step."Rayla, my dear. Always a pleasure to see you." I nodded and sat opposite him. "Confined spaces do you no justice," he sneered. "My finest student. I had such high hopes for you and I still do. I'm sure a host of meditation has done you some good. Mellowed you out a bit"

"I would hope so," I added. Silverado raised an eyebrow. He was using all his energy to read me, and I was using all of mine to block him. Silverado, the man who taught me the fine art of fighting tactics, wasn't memorable to me at all. No flashes came to mind, no memories were churned up as they were with Dayo and the Delights. Nothing. I felt no camaraderie, either. But if I had fought to succumb him, then maybe there wouldn't be much fondness on either side. Damn Delta for wiping my memory. I was likely Diego's greatest disappointment.

"Well Rayla, no point in wasting time. As you recall, I'm a big proponent of dreams, and last night I dreamed about the Crystal Cove," he said, letting the v sound dribble from his lips. "And guess who was sitting in the midst of it? You my dear."

"The Crystal Cove is much like the fountain of youth was to the ancients. We are all in search of this mystical home, and I personally was charged with finding it and uncovering its mysteries. According to my dream, you have accessed it. Problem is, I read through the transcripts for our mind surveillance, watched the recordings of your thoughts and dreams, and it looks like you haven't so much as day-dreamed since you've been in our possession. Even your bedtime dreams are unusually pedestrian. If I didn't know any better, I'd think you were a clone. But that veil of soft skin can't hide the intensity that pulsates beneath it. You are, it appears, human."

"That I am," I added.

"Of course," he said. "So, I would like to make you an offer. We here at Shogun City are open to forgiveness. It is one of the tenets of our planet. It is the reason you are, despite my insistence, alive today. If you lead me to the Crystal Cove, I and the Council Elders have decided to grant you your freedom. But you'll be banned from Planet Hope. Instead, you will live the rest of your years on the planet Earth. "

Earth? Was Ice lighting my path?

"How would I get there?" I asked.

"The strings, of course," he said. "We like to talk as if the Strings are some sort of a fairy tale, but truly if we need to get to Earth and back, believe me we can make it happen. Fortunately, the need hasn't been compelling."

"The Dirk's takeover isn't compelling?" I asked.

"Don't make me laugh, Rayla. Show me how to access the Crystal Cove, and I'll get you to Earth. I don't know how you're getting in there. I don't know if it's meditation, or a slip in consciousness, astral travel, or what; but the Shangos need to be the Cove's protectors. For heaven's sake, we can't let Moulan get access to it. She's done enough."

"Or the The Dirk," I added.

"The who?" he responded, as if he misheard me. "At any rate, give it some thought."

"What will you do once you've accessed it?" I asked.

"You ask too many questions. Your father asked too many questions," he added. Did my father know about the strings, too?

"Just keep it safe from harm," he said. "Keep it safe from rebels like you," he responded. "That is all. And yes, Delta can go with you. He seems to be at your beck and call anyway," Silverado said with a sneer.

"Will you free the people in the caves?" I asked.

"You have such a knack for fiction," said Silverado as he dusted off his lap and rose to exit. He headed for the door.

"I expect that you'll say yes," he said. "I will give you 'til sunrise, and then I must resort to other means," he said. "In your containment, we've become quite sophisticated in extracting information. People here love you so, and we're just not up for the spectacle of it all. Say yes and say yes quickly." His swarthy red cloak swung with the door that shut behind him.

149

Chapter 29

Coltrane Directions

I returned to my bedroom dumbfounded. Earth. My original plan was to get to Earth and recruit help to restore our planet. But that innocent wish seemed so short-sited now. Diva was right about the strings. But is she right about Earth? What good would a trip to Earth do now? Can they even help us? If I get there, could I get back; or would I be like my father and the other astronauts, trapped in time? I'm already trapped in time, I reminded myself.

Either way, I can't give them access to the Crystal Cove. Even if I wanted to, I'm clueless as to how to access it. It's not the kind of thing you hand over to someone. The cove is intangible. Like bottling sunrays or the ether. The whole proposition was ridiculous. This equitable exchange was a joke. I recounted the story to Delta.

"Do you know anyone else who has been to the Cove?" I asked Delta.

"No," he said. "You're the only one. Besides, real intuits don't need spaceships," he quipped, his eyes sparkling with his trademark twinkle. So he was reading my mind.

"The Neo Astronauts were lost because they tried to go to different planets, unfamiliar territory that were repositories for other lifetimes, but their travel to Earth in real time worked just fine," I said. "My father went to Earth and returned with no problem." Then it hit me. "Delta, do you think that the rest of the Neo Astronauts are on modern-day Earth?" I asked. I thought of the messages from the Crystal Cove that we picked up in Washington, D.C.

"It's possible," he said. "The only way to be sure is to get there."

"Maybe something or someone is preventing them from returning," I said.

"Or maybe there's nothing to return to," he said.

I ignored Delta's stinging comment. I didn't know what to make of it, yet I was lasering in to traveling to Earth.

"We'll go tonight," I said.

"What are you waiting for?" Delta asked me. "You've been asleep long enough."

I took Delta's hand. I recounted all that Moulan had taught us about focus. I held an image of my father seared in my mind. I thought of the Neo Astronauts on that mountain many years ago holding hands, looking to the sky. I remembered the beaming glee and excitement of our world on the brink of innovation. I remembered Sui Lee holding my hand, keeping me from joining the circle. I tried to remember the moment before they disappeared, the swirling sensation, the lightheaded feeling and the brightly lit sun expanding. I thought of Notia and my wishes for her escape on the flying ark. I will find my spaceship. Then it all went black.

How will we find them, I wondered? Then I answered myself: They'll find us.

"If you're lost and you look then you will find me."

– Cindi Lauper, Earth, 1984

***

I could see the rising Earth before us through the front window of the ship. Delta, my copilot, took my hand, and I downshifted gears as we entered this foreign atmosphere much like my own. This was the home of my ancestors. This ancient planet was the birthplace of my civilization. Our ship was undetectable and nearly invisible to most human eyes. Delta and I landed softly in a body of blue water, one lake of five in what Ice recounted as her home—The United States of America.

No one saw us come out of the water. No one saw us walk to shore. A few children with short pants ran along the beach pulling a kite. They didn't notice us either. This area of the shore was fairly isolated. I noticed a tall, blue-haired woman disappear behind an ancient stone structure that stood in the distance, and that's when we spotted the flying vehicles, whizzing by at low altitudes, with towering buildings, new and ancient, scraping the horizon.

This was not Planet Hope. For one, once we crossed the road along the yellow shore, the city was swarming with people, each zipping with their eyes forward as they raced to their destinations, somewhat reminiscent of the people in the caves. The flying vehicles above sped by with reckless abandon; and twice, Delta and I ducked when flying cars dipped too low. We walked slowly, each deliberate step screaming visitor, and turned off into a less dense corridor with slower-walking people. A short man with a round face, orange body suit, and warm eyes stared at us.

"Are y'all from Mars?" he asked. Delta and I looked at one another. His accent was ancient; one I recalled hearing in a childhood lesson. It had a song-like rhythm that reminded me of the one in Washington, D.C., in my other life. Mars, if my memory served correctly, was the name of the red planet and neighbor to Earth, the one we whizzed by before passing Earth's moon.

"Why do you ask?" I said.

"My cousin went to Lil L.A. on Mars once, said everybody was wearing those shiny, steel-toed boots," he said. "But theirs are red and come up to your thigh," he said. I looked from my boots to his thin-soled brown slippers with a strip between his toes and noted the difference.

"You from one of them Space Stations?" he asked. "I've never been to em', but I watch that dance show they do on Emerald Isle, where everybody moves real fast. A lot of pretty ladies on Emerald Isle."

"We're from Planet Hope," said Delta.

The man doubled over laughing. I don't know what we expected with our proclamation. In fact, I don't know why Delta shared anything at all. I didn't get the sense that this laughing man was someone to guard against. I wasn't sure if he could be of much help either. He called over to a tall woman, with bright blue hair pulled back into a ponytail, leaning against a metal beam. Was this the woman I noticed on the yellow sand?

"Luba, these folks say they're from Planet Hope."

"Really," she said, her words dripped slowly like the sap from the trees of the Enchanted Forest. "The land of no return, hmmmm," the blue-haired one said.

"Might as well say you're from Atlantis," the man said. I didn't get the comparison. Ice taught that Atlantis was a thriving culture before its demise. Was he trying to say that Planet Hope was no more? "See any dragons and unicorns along the way?" he said, chuckling to the point of coughing. Why would we see dragons and unicorns? I wondered. "That's a good one, son," he said, wiping his brow as he cleared his throat.

I never thought about Earth and their thoughts on Planet Hope. With so little contact over the years, modern-day Earth could have forgotten our existence, like the Earth people had forgotten about Atlantis. The thought made me shiver. Impossible, I thought. But I could sense that Delta was thinking the same thing. The man and his blue-haired pal moved on.

I followed them.

"We don't want no trouble," the man said as I drew closer.

"We're not looking for any. Can you tell me about Planet Hope?" I asked.

"She's serious," the man said to Luba. The two exchanged glances.

"Looks like you came a ways," Luba said shyly, her dark brown eyes swallowing us all whole. "Invite them to one of your big dinners," she said. He sighed. Luba didn't have to do much convincing. He was obviously smitten.

"Well, if you really want to know, we have a pal, a guy named Suni who's really into that distant star stuff. He's travelled around our solar system a bit. Met some weird people along the way. You'd be up his cosway. He's havin' dinner with us, if you wanna join."

The man's name was Charlie, but he asked us to call him Chase. Chase said that he and Luba were of the old world. "All we need is a fishin' pole, 3D virtual reality port, a Wi-Fi internet connection, and a sturdy flying electric car. The simple life," he said. He lived in an old, small house within walking distance from the greenish blue lake. The brick and mortar building was sturdy and quaint.

"This here building is 250 years old," said Charlie. "Made it after the second world war. They call it a bungalow. Only a handful of em' left in the world." Chase had an organic farm in his backyard. He traded food for services, he said. Luba was a dancer who performed at a club in the heart of the city. "Luba's always droppin' by for my green apples," he said. Suni was a guard there. Chase, I suppose, was a frequent patron.

We each sat at the table as Chase fixed our plates. I'd seen most of the foods before. Carrots, peas, cabbage, collard greens. But there were others, sweet foods with crème toppings that were totally foreign.

"We're a people that believes in sugar," said Chase. "I don't care how illegal it is," he said. He showed me images of other family members on his tablet. Some lived in the area, but most moved to the space stations for work, Chase said. He wasn't married anymore. Dated a virtual girl for a few years who introduced him to Luba's avatar. They both had an affinity for homegrown food, he said. But Chase didn't plan on leaving Earth any time soon.

"I just couldn't get used to floating around all the time," he said. "You don't float around on all of 'em" Luba interjected. "He's so old world," she whispered. A knock at the door interrupted us. Luba answered the door and Suni entered. Suni was a well-chiseled man with a twinkle in his eye. His dark hair fell to his shoulders, and he wore an all blue ensemble. His warm demeanor didn't belie his strength. Delta and I could handle him with ease if it got to that point, but we weren't worried. He greeted Delta and I with a smile. Chase made the introductions.

"This here is my new buddies," he said. "They've come a ways and got a real interest in Planet Hope."

"Where are you from?" he asked.

"We're from Planet Hope," I told him. Suni paused briefly, shock consumed his face. Suni flashed a grin.

"Welcome," he said, as he took a seat at the dinner table. Luba blessed the food and we ate.

"How long you been here?" Suni asked.

"We just arrived," said Delta.

"You don't know how you got here, do you?" he asked.

Chase chuckled again. He laughed hysterically before nearly choking on a spoonful of corn. Luba assisted him.

"Chase here is laughing because Planet Hope, by most people's accounts, was a failed project. You go around and tell others you're from Planet Hope, and you might find yourself locked away or kicked out the solar system," he said.

"What do you know?" I asked.

"A long time ago, a host of people signed up for a mission to a distant star and others were sent away as punishment. Some of the best and worst minds of this planet headed that way. The project had a no-return policy. It took so long to get out there at that time, and it wasn't so easy to get back. It was supposed to be like paradise, a place where precious stones and metals were like pebbles scattered across the planet. That was the rumor. There was contact the first few decades, then there was nothing. No one ever heard from them again. Then one day, astronomers couldn't even find the planet on the map. Said a star exploded or something like that. Caused a panic. Earth downsized their space operations,

154

concentrating on more space stations and recalibrating atmospheres on moons within our solar system. All part of the galactic alliance, a broader coalition of societies falling within Earth's jurisdiction. But a lot of people thought the whole Planet Hope project was fishy. Some said it was an eradication program. Others said the people were enslaved. Others said the whole thing was a hoax. But the more adventurous of us wanted to go out there and see for ourselves. Me and a couple of guys went for it, tried to go beyond the jurisdiction, and got yanked back so fast by some galactic forces. They scared the crap out of us. Threatened to take our interplanetary passports."

"I told ya," Chase said, chuckling. "Like chasing a pot of gold at the end of a rainbow." Luba nudged him, and he stopped laughing and began choking again. She escorted him into a neighboring room. Years of no contact made us a myth.

"We're very much alive," I said. "We were a colony that went independent. It was a struggle because Earth wanted to be in command, but we wanted our own life," I said. "Our own ways."

"That could be so," he said. "But the masses of people on this end of the galaxy didn't know about your struggle. Some would say you don't even exist."

"You're not from Earth," said Delta.

"I was born on Mars. My family came from Malaysia on Earth and settled around Red City five generations ago. We lived outside of the main city. It was a nice place, strong community. But I wanted adventure and set out to hitchhike across the solar system when I was 18. I've been all over. Most of the 150 space stations, all the continents on Earth—Titan, Europa, some moons around Pluto. And of course, you heard about my attempt to get near Planet Hope."

"So you've never been beyond this solar system?" asked Delta.

"I flew beyond to other spots in the galaxy. I worked as crew on an explorer ship looking to mine asteroids. Heard a lot of off-color stories, saw some unexplainable things. And I can tell by looking at you that you're not from any of the worlds I've been to." Luba returned to join us. She slipped into her seat, propping both elbows on the table; as she placed her chin on her hands, a few strands of blue hair fell in her face. She reminded me of someone. "Chase is resting," she said in her song-like voice. Luba, it seemed, didn't want to miss the story.

Suni was skeptical of us. A trained guard and hardened traveler, he was watchful but he kept talking anyway. Whether curiosity had the best of him or he loved a captive audience, I wasn't sure. Either way, Delta and I were eager listeners.

"I met a woman at a bar on Titan. She claimed she was from Planet Hope. Her name was Eartha Mandela. She was trying to hitch a ride back to Earth. Wanted to meet with officials. Had a similar story to you, except she said she was an astronaut and they were traveling with their minds. Kind woman, very rattled, though. Her story was plum crazy. Said she could travel with her mind. Said she'd been to Earth, but that those who remained on her crew sent her out to get to Planet Hope. She got a ship, got as far as Titan, and the ship broke down. She couldn't repair it. I took a look at it, but even if I could repair it, she couldn't make it as far as Planet Hope, not with those galactic troops around. Not to mention that Planet Hope didn't even exist, as far as I was concerned. I snuck her onto my ship and dropped her off not too far from here. She said her crew was in Chicagotropolis. She had no I.D., nothing. Scanners couldn't pull up any records on her. I told her she could stay with me for a while, but she declined. "Luba, you remember her? I brought her to the club a long time ago. Really pretty lady," he said.   You bring a lot of pretty ladies around," Luba said.

Suni continued. "Haven't seen her since. But she was dressed kind of like you."

The Neo Astronauts were here.

"How long ago was that?" Delta asked.

"Bout 8 years ago," he said.

"We're looking for the Neo Astronauts," I said. "Eartha sounds like she was one of them."

"Well let me warn you," he said. "I know people went there and all, but the authorities out this way say it exploded, and most of the people have bought into it. If your friends got close to any of the ruling parties out here, they wouldn't get a kind welcoming. At the very least, they'd have a lot of convincing to do."

I appreciated Suni's forthrightness, but I couldn't believe that all of Earth's people thought Planet Hope was a failure. Did our independence cause a rift between Earth's leaders and ours? Was the rift permanent? Was that the real reason Planet Hope rarely travelled to Earth? This side of the story wasn't taught when I was a child, and it's a matter I hadn't thought about. What about the families of those who went away? Surely some of them would be curious about their loved ones, but Earth hadn't mastered eternal youth yet. Could that pose a problem? The first inhabitant had left nearly 200 years ago, or was it longer? "What year is this?" I asked.

"2212. This here is Chicagotropolis. You are in the US of A."

Chicago. That's where Ice said her family was from. If I could find some of my relatives or the relatives of the Neo Astronauts, would I find the Neo Astronauts themselves?

"Do you remember anything else?" I asked. "Anything she said?"

"She kept talking about some guy named Kent. Said he was the leader. Said she wanted to contact him."

My father, Kent Illmatic?

"Was Kent with her crew?" I asked.

"I'm not sure. Really pretty lady. She really missed some kid of hers, too. Kid's name was uh ..."

"Delta," Delta said softly.

"Yeah, that's it."

Delta stood abruptly.

"Looks like we're in the right place," he said. "Thanks for your time."

I wasn't ready to leave yet, but Delta was deeply disturbed. Delta, I'd almost forgotten, was the only surviving child of the Neo Astronauts, too. Another bond we shared.

"I'll be outside," he said. Delta exited the front door.

"Did I say something wrong?" Suni said.

"No, not at all."

"Is it true that planet has everlasting life?" he asked. "We've deconstructed age, ended the process," I said.

"Just like the clan said," Luba said. What clan? I wondered, but I didn't ask. There was a power dynamic at play; and Luba, for the time being, could only say so much. Suni nodded, pondering my claims. Suni didn't necessarily believe my origins, but he was convinced that I believed them, which was satisfying enough for him.

"How in the hell did you get here?" he asked.

I could try to explain the techniques. I could try to explain how we would go up in an invisible ship. But the experience was beyond words, beyond logic; but even the most elementary explanation, I felt, was beyond Suni's comprehension. This place, it seemed, was still stuck on the 3rd dimension.

"Same way Eartha did," I said.

"Is it really like paradise?" Luba asked, her round eyes peppered with hope.

"I'm here to ensure that we get back to that point," I said.

Chase emerged in a stupor of some kind.

"Suni, you done with them stories? Come check out what I did with that peppercorn you found."

Suni excused himself and headed for the backdoor with Chase before turning around.

"I hope what I said helped," he said meekly.

"Very much so," I said. He left out, the door slamming behind him.

So the Neo Astronauts had landed in this area. Moulan, for all her follies, did something right. My father had trekked this land. I could feel him in the atmosphere. Could this be it? I was totally immersed in thought, when I noticed Luba staring at me. We were alone.

"I know some people who believe in Planet Hope," she said quietly. "I can take you to em' if you want."

"Who are they?" I asked. "Just some believers," she said. "I met them at the club," she said. She looked behind her to be sure that the guys were away. "They're among the Outkast," she said. "They're followers of Ice," she added. Could she be talking about Ice of Planet Hope? She answered my question before I could ask it.

"Ice Ostara, the goddess that oversees space and time travelers, love in other dimensions."

"Ice is a spirit guide on my planet," I said. "She was born here."

"We know," she said.

"She was my father's mother," I said.

Luba didn't respond. Did she believe me? Had these Outkasts met the Neo Astronauts?

"I'll take you to them, but I'll need something in return," she said.

158

"What?" I asked.

"I want to go with you, back to Planet Hope" she said. "I've never left the planet before. I can help," she said, pleading her case. "I know these city streets. I know the surrounding town. I know the planet, and I can tell ya don't know that."

She was right. But I didn't need convincing. I don't know what came over me, but the thought of someone feeling trapped was a feeling I knew too well. If she believed in Ice, then we were sisters in time.

"You can come with us," I said. "But this won't be an easy journey." She smiled and ran to the back window.

"I'll be back in a few," she said, grabbed a few green apples off the table, tossed them in a bag she grabbed behind the couch, and nodded that she was ready.

"I've been waiting for this day to come," she said sheepishly.

Chapter 30

Rebel Like Grace Jones

DELTA was on the porch, smoking his smelly stick. He looked from me to Luba in utter confusion, one only evident with the furrow of an eyebrow. His effervescent cool remained, but he didn't ask any questions. "Welcome to team Planet Hope," he said to Luba. "Only the bravest among you get to hang with us. Hope you don't mind the smoke," he said. And the three of us walked briskly in the opposite direction of the setting sun, towards the post where Luba said the Outkast lived. I hadn't had the camaraderie of the sisterhood in sometime, and I was glad Luba came along. But there was something familiar about her.

Luba said that travelling by foot was best. "No one pays much attention to what goes on here on the ground," she said. We didn't have licenses to be in the air either, she said, and didn't want to tip off patrols. Most of the city dwellers lived in towers, she said. The richer they were, the higher they lived, she added. The Outkast and those who sought a quieter life stayed closer to the earth's surface, below the crowded air traffic above. "They don't care if you have ID down here," she said. There was no clear road, and she suggested we cut through an abandoned area of the old side of town city that was overgrown with green life.

Luba was from a town called Kingston, a metropolis on an island south of the U.S. A lot of her hometown friends had jobs in space tourism, but Luba had other dreams. She came this way a few years ago, hoping to work her way up and live on Emerald Isle, a space station on the dark side of the moon. She got as high as the 290th floor, or the club where she worked.

"It's really hard getting off this planet," she said, as we marched through the grass. "If you don't have a visa, you need travel clearance, or currency," she said. "Hard currency is hard to come by. But I have other ways," she said.

We walked beyond the concrete floors of the city through the outskirts and their tall reeds. I thought of the Field of the Golden Lady and the fear that gripped my heart as I ran in search of Moulan Shakur. I was many light-years away from that fear now, literally in a world apart, the world of my ancestors, the world Carcine charged me to find. We passed the green fields into the last vestiges of an old city, dilapidated buildings, worn signs and postings, but no people.

"This is the abandoned city," Luba said. "There are many of them. People left for the cities in the sky," she said. "If they could." We passed through this small town, the ghosts of yesteryear hung over the city streets. Did the yearning for living beyond Earth's atmosphere cause the blight in this city? I wondered. Was society always looking for a better way, a new way, and disavowing the old only to recreate the same scenarios again? We continued walking; I whispered to Delta.

"What are you thinking?" I asked.

"I'm just taking it all in," he said. "This place has a different energy, and I'm just trying to read it," he said.

"We're close," I told Delta.

"We wouldn't be here otherwise," he added.

According to Luba, the Outkasts were a group of misfits who pulled away from society to find their own way. They preferred the low-tech life, lived secretly, and created their own society away from the big cities. These abandoned cities were their playground, and they had adopted one as their primary post. While everyone else was striving to get off the planet, this group was firmly rooted in the terra. They were also, by most accounts, unplugged. There were other low-tech groups, she said, but the Outkast were especially unique because of their celebration of Ice Ostara and their rumored Temple of Sound.

"What's the Temple of Sound?" I asked.

"I'll let them explain," she said.

The ways and lives of the Outkasts were so secretive that few knew anything about them, if they knew of their existence at all.

"Are you an Outkast?" I asked her.

"No," she said as we marched forward. "I am not a descendent of anyone who went to Planet Hope. That belief, in this world, makes one an Outkast. Most people here are convinced that Planet Hope did not exist." We stopped in front of an iron building, some 40 feet tall. I couldn't get a read on the building.

"They're usually in here," she said. A woman with long, thick red braids and a weapon at her side came out.

"Is this them?" the woman said.

"Yes," Luba said. Luba had communicated with the base telepathically. It explained why she didn't have any communication devices, but how did I miss it?

"We're very happy to have you," the woman said. "I'm Aponi," she said. "Welcome to the base of the Outkasts. Welcome to the new Earth."

We entered. The inside was some kind of a high-tech generator. A dozen or so people sat around the perimeter. A man with white, short, tightly curled hair and dimples stood.

"I'm Martin," the man said. "Are you from Planet Hope?" he asked.

"Yes," I said. The others on the perimeter looked to one another. Martin's gaze was steady.

"Is your name, Rayla?" he asked.

"Yes," I said.

"And you're Delta, I assume," he said. Delta nodded. Delta was sizing up the scene.

"My grandfather was among the first to go to Planet Hope. His name was Mongo Santamaria. He was part of the global lottery and was one of the few Cuban citizens to go. His girlfriend, my grandmother, was pregnant at the time, but did not realize it until he'd left. He emailed stories and photos. She applied for the lottery each year, but didn't make it. The story goes that, after ten years, she lost all contact. Then the government announced that their star exploded. But we knew there were survivors. My grandmother believed it, and I believe it, too. Most of us here in this room had ancestors who went to Planet Hope. Despite all that's happened, we knew that one day the children of Planet Hope would return. We've been looking for you."

"Did you know of Mongo Santamaria?" he asked.

"No, I did not," I said, quickly regretting what I'd said. Martin's smile withered a bit. "Perhaps he knew my grandmother, Ice Ostara," I said. The others looked at one another and back at me.

"We're looking for others who were here. Astronauts," I said. "Kent Illmatic, Eartha Mandela.

"You claim Ice Ostara as your own?" Martin said.

"Yes," I proclaimed.

"Planet Hope. A land of such promise. The fables say that you had the best of the best. The best technology, schools, ecosystems, scientists, metaphysicians. But you don't look like scientists," he said. "And you don't act like mystics. My training tells me that you're militia. Shogun militia. And if you are, in fact, claiming Ice Ostara, you will have to prove it."

The others along the perimeter stood. I estimated about 10. We were surrounded.

"Martin, they are friends," Luba pleaded.

"Then let them prove it," he said. Martin reached for a silver firing arm at his hip, but Delta's lightening quick blow struck the weapon from his hands. They each reached for their weapons, but all were too slow. And as Delta and I aimed and slashed, we went for the nonfatal blows. I did not want to kill these people; these believers who held out so much promise for their ancestors were not the enemy. Only Aponi was able to fire her weapon; but by the time she did, her partners were unarmed and floored. I dodged her bullet, and it shattered a large square mirror on the wall. I tackled and unarmed her in a single swoop. Delta had Martin pinned.

"Enough," a man's voice yelled. I knew this voice. The scratchy depth of another time, another place whose confusion was my stability. But it couldn't be.

"Carcine," I said. I loosened my grip on Aponi and looked up. Carcine stood above the carnage. His clothes clang to him, worn with time. He wore a short grey cloak and the boots I last saw him in. His hair was blue and long. He tossed off his jacket, and Luba ran to him throwing her arms around him.

That should have been me.

"Hello, Rayla," he said. "You've found me."

With Luba's arms around Carcine and Delta at my side, I was frozen. I didn't know what to think or feel. What should have been happiness was a pillar of salt that I leaned on to offset the shock. The Outkast, withered in pain as they rolled about the floor.

"Greetings, Delta," he said. "It's been a while." Delta said nothing. He kept his knee at Martin's throat.

Carcine stepped over the wounded, a smile creeped on his face. He moved past his crew and kissed me lightly on the cheek.

"I am very happy to see you," he said, as if he'd seen me yesterday for tea. Maybe in this world he had.

"You've met Luba," he said.

"Yes," I responded. I looked to Delta and his eyes were deadest on Carcine.

I suppose this was our time.

Chapter 31

The Harder They Go

CARCINE invited Delta and I into his chamber, a small grey room with a silver square table, wooden chairs, and a bright red carpet. I could see my reflection on the table surface, and a silver chandelier hung at the room's center. Carcine sat on one side of the table, Delta and me on the other. A fruit basket with lush mangos divided us, and Carcine served us all some spicy red tonic water. "We made it ourselves," he said, as we toasted with the dark liquid he was so proud of. Carcine was all smiles. I was wary, and Delta was watchful. I did not know this new Carcine. I studied Carcine's face, looking for a hint of familiarity in his deep-set eyes. This man whom I had loved, just moments before, had his forces try to kill me.

"Your welcoming committee needs better fighting skills," I said. Carcine smiled, devishly.

"I had to be sure it was you," he said. "Luba was convinced. I was not, until now."

"How could you not recognize me?" I demanded.

"I didn't expect you to come with a friend," he said with a smile. Bastard, I thought, but I remained focused. Delta leaned back in his chair; Carcine ignored him.

"Luba found me. I woke up on these yellow shores completely unaware of how I got here. When I came here, these people, the Outkasts, already believed in Ice," he said. "When I proved that I was from Planet Hope, just as you

165

did, they took me in. But there are other sightings of people from our home, people who've come before. Follow me," he said, as he stood and exited a side door. Delta and I followed, but before we left, Delta took my hand.

"Remember who you are, Rayla. This is not the time to forget," he said. I nodded, and we moved on.

Carcine walked us into a large chamber, some kind of a communication center. A few of the Outkasts were inside, pecking away on an ancient keyboard. Panels of metal created an arc structure.

"We use this to pick up on sound waves, new energy blips that come into the atmosphere," he said.

"A surveillance chamber?" I asked, thinking of the Dirk and Shango monitoring system.

"That would be totally unnecessary," he said. "This is more like a satellite, where we communicate with extraterrestrial life or life beyond this galaxy, new life entering this galaxy. We're aliens on this Planet. It's a bit primitive, but we've picked up messages from other times, maybe other spaces," he said.

Flashback. I remember my life in D.C., the device that the rebels had, the message with my name.

"You sent me a message," I said.

"No," he responded. "I didn't build this," he added. "This center was here when I got here. The Outkasts say it has been with them for some time." Then who sent the message, I wondered. I rubbed my hand along the metallic surface and stopped when my hands hit groove marks. It read "Illmatic." Did my father send the message?

"That name is scribbled all over this thing," said Carcine. "Could be your dad, or just some fan of ancient rap music."

"I saw a prototype of this before," I said. "You did, too. Do you remember?" I asked Carcine.

"I don't have the capacity for memory that you do," he said. "That's not my gift. I just take it one life at a time." Carcine's dismissiveness was unnecessary. Delta surveyed the area, the floating data images were clouds hanging above our heads. Carcine watched him closely.

"You don't like what you see, Delta?" Carcine asked.

"Just looking," Delta said, peering into a giant metallic pit. "This is a landing station," Delta said.

"You have good eyes," said Carcine. "It was designed by someone as a portal as well. A place for those lost to Planet Hope to return. Not sure how it works, but the people say that the son of Ice built it." Kent Illmatic. I noticed the familiar ancient etchings on the wall, the same old writings that lined the Crystal Cove. I ran my finger along the grooves of the unreadable words in the cave wall. "My father sent those messages in D.C. What language is this?" I asked.

"No one knows," said Carcine. I wanted the others to leave and to be alone in this cave. Could this be the Crystal Cove? I pressed my body to the cave's warm walls, closed my eyes, and felt the pulse of the universe. Could this be it? But where are the crystals? My hand ran across a gold plate. A light flickered. Delta looked to the light fixtures.

"You breaking things, Illmatic?" Delta asked.

The Crystal Cove was a time portal, a racetrack from one universe to the next, from one time to another. Could the strings that The Shangos spoke of lead here? Was this what Moulan was aiming to protect? But it was locked in some way. Did these people know what they had? We returned to the room with the fruit basket and took our seats. Carcine poured more spicy tonic and passed it to us.

"You're guarding the Crystal Cove," I said. "We need to unlock it."

"I don't know much about that," Carcine chirped. "The who, how, and whys this thing was created isn't my concern," he said. "I'm glad you two made it through. Saw you arriving through our radar. But I've got another mission."

"Which is what?" I asked.

"Isn't it obvious," he said. "It's a revolution. The restoration of humanity on this planet and the next. You saw those cities—the division, the dirty, and the scum. We can't leave our planet of origin in such shape."

"What about Planet Hope?" I said.

"What about it?" he asked.

"At one point you were fighting to restore our home," I said.

"Home," he said. "That's an interesting way of looking at it. Isn't this home, too?" he asked. "Home is where the heart is," he reminded me. "Where is your heart, Rayla Illmatic?"

What was Carcine saying?

"What happened when you left the camp to find Moulan?" I asked.

"I never found her," he said. "I guess she was a myth. I came back to the camp and you'd left," he said. What kind of twisted madness had Carcine bought into?

"No, that's not what happened," I said. "You disappeared." We were together in Moulan's world. Had he forgotten? "You told me to find you in three days," I said.

"And I came back in four," he replied. No, impossible, I thought.

"Then how did you get here?" I asked.

"How did you get here?" he asked. "Here, there, does it matter? We're fighting, traveling through space and time. Does it really matter where I am when one is fighting for justice?"

"You said that this was not our time and you vanished," I said, my voice barely above a whisper. I swallowed my confusion. Carcine took a deep breath and sighed.

I didn't understand his bout of arrogance. Why was he doing this to me? Or was I doing this to myself?

"I need you to come back with us and help us," but before I could continue, Carcine began laughing.

"Rayla, open your eyes. Do you see a theme here? You're world hopping and dealing with the same struggle—the same perpetual motion that we faced on Planet Hope. Who's the common denominator in this experience?" he asked.

"I am," I said.

"I left to find you," I said, but even I knew that my journey had taken me beyond Carcine's reach. I expected my heart to break, but it did not. I looked at Carcine, studied his hollow eyes. Delta interrupted. "We all make choices, Carcine."

"That we do, Delta," said Carcine.

"Where are the Neo Astronauts?" Delta continued, trying to get the conversation refocused.

"Delta, you of all people can't be serious. You know exactly where they are. Where they want to be. Just like we all are. Just like you are. This is about more than us. To the struggle," he said, taking another swig from his cup.

"Didn't you hear the man tell you that our star exploded," Carcine said. "There is no Planet Hope."

"I don't believe that," I said.

"Then you explain where we are?" he barked. "You explain this time lapse, the inability to leave the planet, the lost people, and the stretch in time. We are ghosts of the cosmos, and Delta here is too afraid to tell you."

"That's not true," I said. "You've been poisoned by this world. You're confused," I said. "Am I?" he said. "I'm sorry you came all this way to discover this," he said. "I'm sure it was as difficult for the others, too."

"The Neo Astronauts?" I said.

"Who else," he added. "They're powerful folks, but they can't rebuild a star."

"And you haven't seen them?" Delta asked.

"I keep these boots in case they come around. The Outkasts and that satellite are monitors just in case. Others have spotted them in the past. Kent even inspired a movie. They're legends in this world."

"And what are you?" I asked.

"I'm just a man," he said.

Carcine wallowed in hopelessness. He'd forgotten our planet. He forgot me. This reconnection was not what I'd hoped, but Carcine and I were different people. I was claiming my power, and he was not. "These legends you mentioned," I said, trying to say focused, "where can I find them?"

Carcine called for Aponi. "Aponi knows them. They were real popular in her hometown."

I could ask more questions, but it was pointless. I wanted to rescue him, to save him from himself. But Carcine, for some reason, had traded our fight at home, for a class war with lower stakes in this one. He was completely clueless about the Crystal Cove, not realizing that his very presence was protecting it. He was trapped in the web of impossibilities and content with the fight for the sake of the fight. He'd lost hope. He'd lost me. I walked out, leaving him to his four-walled prison. Ice must be protecting me from myself. Another me in another time would have split in two.

Chapter 32

Doves With Pride

CARCINE and I joined Aponi outside. She'd lit a campfire that blazed in the setting sun. She had some sort of monitoring device where she could project images into the air, as if she were flashing onto those old-world screens. One was a flying man with a sheet on his back from a planet that had been destroyed. He hid amongst the people and surfaced for heroic feats. His identity was hidden. Another draped a mask across his face, riding a white horse and some large hat, after his friends were sabotaged and he was rescued. He went on to help others, going from town to town as a masked man. Another was a woman who came from an island of women, the Enchanted Forest perhaps, and rode invisible planes like ours, arresting villains with her strength and beauty. One was a king who came from another country like Ku and dawned the semblance of a panther as he restored the world. One woman used powers of the sea, taking on the image of a mermaid. Another lived in molten lava, using her passion to inspire the world. But these were stories Ice had shared. One even disguised herself as a miniature version of herself, grew wings, and flew. These weren't stories of the lost astronauts, or were they? Were there any clues in these long tales at all? Luba joined us, looked at the flashing images.

"Maybe they'll write one about you. About us. About this," I said.

"Why not?" Delta said. "This land is filled with colorful characters. And you, my love, are a rainbow." A smile crept across my face. My first true smile on this journey. Delta was unusually silent during this trip. I wondered what he was thinking. But before I could ask, he posed the same question. "What do you think?" Delta asked.

"I think that Planet Hope is alive and that the Neo Astronauts are within reach," I said. "I think that cave we were in was a replica of the Crystal Cove, one built around the technology of the rebels in D.C., but not the cove itself. It was created by Kent Illmatic himself. "

"So you haven't lost faith," he said.

"Never," I affirmed.

"Good," he said. "I'd hate to waste such a milestone of a trip," he said. "Rayla, I'm sorry about the things that Carcine said," Delta stated, referring to Carcine and his forgetfulness. "Everyone isn't up for the path you've chosen." He looked away not quite sure of his next words. "I know that you love him," he said. "And if it weren't for his charge, we wouldn't be here now," he said.

But there was no point in regret. I looked Delta square in his light brown eyes. "Never say those words to me again. There is nothing for either of us to feel sorry about," I quipped, before leaning in and kissing him. Our lips met for what felt like eternity. Then I stepped back, and we continued walking.

Think, think, think, I told myself as Delta and I walked the camp in silence. But thinking was not the solution. I needed to be, be one with myself, this new nature and gritty city about me and tap into the energy of my ancestors—the ones who lived lives both remembered and forgotten on this distant planet. The ones whose life created my own. Moulan, at some point in time, had mastered many energies because she came to this land, this place. There was magic here. There was life, and there was love for life. Ice had come from this land of conflict and beauty, this imperfect world with the seeds of its best to create our Planet Hope. She was molded by its irony and allure. Those seeds were here, and I would feed off of them to find the Missing, to find my father. I needed to free myself of logic and pensive concentration. And for some reason going into this relic of the Crystal Cove didn't make any sense. I didn't need the air of these isolated retreats. I needed the pulsating air of the bustling city. Kent Illmatic was born in Obama City, the most exciting city in the galaxy, even by Shogun standards. Kent would be in the heart of the city. I spotted Luba, posted with Aponi by a wooden barricade. "Luba," I said. "What is the name of that club you mentioned?" I asked.

"Rhiannon," she said. I always liked the letter R, always adored the raaaaa sound. My heart chakra lit up just thinking about it.

"I would like to go there," I said.

"I knew you would," she chimed.

Chapter 33

Everybody in the Mask Turn it Up

LUBA admitted that the blue-haired woman I imagined by the lake was her. She had a dream about two snakes diving from the sky into the water and emerging with a cobra crown the week of our arrival. She alerted Carcine, who confirmed that it appeared an untraceable ship was coming in off coordinates that linked to where Planet Hope would be. "He was expecting one," she said. Luba had a similar dream when Carcine arrived, too. But she hadn't seen the Neo Astronauts.

Rhiannon was celebrating its seventh anniversary tonight. The place was the destination for the unusual, powerful, and the eccentric, said Luba. Most of the regulars were savvy interstellar travelers. We would be her guests, but we had to adjust to the night's celebratory theme and wear a mask.

"It's a masked ball," she said. "A party," she affirmed.

"I don't want to wear a mask," I said, thinking of those masked heroes in the stories I watched.

"Well, you have to," Luba said. We were in Luba's tiny home, a stone's throw away from the Outkasts and Carcine. Her place was draped with bright clothes and accents that sparkled in every gradation of shiny that existed. To my surprise, she had a closet full of masks of all shapes and sizes, from lavish feathers to dainty porcelain, heavy wood to shimmering fabric. Luba, it seemed, had more masks than she could count.

"Why do you have so many?" I asked her. Why did she have any at all?

"I lose myself in them and become more of me in the process," she said. "It's a game I've grown accustomed to."

I could relate. Delta wasn't paying us much attention, sizing up Luba's elaborate knife collection.

"May I?" he asked. Luba nodded. Delta lifted a 9-inch knife with a silver tiger-claw handle. He flipped it over in his hands. Then he picked up another with a twisted snake handle and a turquoise stone embedded in the middle. The handle matched our necklace.

"I'm a collector," she said sheepishly, her eyes darting from me to Delta. I left the pile of masks and glided nearly mesmerized to the knife. Delta handed it to me.

"Where did you get this?" I asked.

"Do you recognize it?" she asked.

I placed my hand on my chest, lifting the necklace for her to see.

"My mother told me a story. A long, long time ago, there was a princess in what is now Eritrea, the only heir to the thrown and the first woman guardian of the cove. Most questioned whether she was ready. She was so young, she was a woman, and her role would defy tradition. She was going to marry a prince from nearby, but on their wedding day an ark came out of the sky and took her and several others with her. The Crystal Cove went with her. The people were sad, but they knew that she would protect it on her journeys, that she was protecting them and one day she would return. You are here. You are the Guardian of the Crystal Cove," she said, her eyes brightened and she threw her hands over her mouth and screamed. She regained her composure. "And you," she, pointing to Delta. "You're her protector." She threw her hands over her mouth again, removed them and sighed.

"Not much is left from that time, but this belonged to her, your family. As you can imagine, much has happened since those days, but some of us centuries later were at least able to recover some things. A relative of mine was assisting an archeologist and stumbled upon it in the black market," she said. "He almost paid for the knife with his life, but he was able to smuggle it and bring it home. They trusted me to keep it. They knew that if anyone could make it off the planet, to get closer to the other guardian, it would be me. They made me a guardian. It was mine, but now it is yours," she said, handing it to me."

The story of that other life reminded me of my best friend Notia. Notia was my only true woman friend. Luba reminded me of her. Now I know why. Had I returned? Was I a myth?

173

"I don't know about any Neo Astronauts. But I know that you are the Guardian of the Crystal Cove. If you believe your friends from the ark are here, then they are here. Rhiannon has no idea that they have a special guest in tow." I held the knife in my hand. Delta was not phased by Luba's glee, as if he knew this all along. I had gripped this handle before. Luba hopped back into the closet, rustling through her piles of masks.

"You must pick one, Rayla," Luba said. "One that's fitting of your return." I sifted through Luba's menagerie of masks. I picked a shimmering silver mask with tiny pearls that dangled on the side, a turquoise blue feather headdress accompanied it.

"I like turquoise," I said.

"Yes," she said. Luba pointed to a trunk of gowns. While I liked them all, they weren't ideal for battle. One must always be prepared.

"Do you have anything else?" I asked.

"We will make something," she said. With that, Luba pulled out another trunk of fabrics. She cut and stitched, measured and primped, as Delta sifted through her unusual outfits for men. Delta settled on a black helmet with a red strip of fur up the middle.

"I'm a unicorn," he miffed.

Luba assembled a red fitted gown with no straps. She handed me a blue fitted body suit to wear under it.

"Yes," she said looking us over. "We are ready. You are ready. I will get Carcine," she said.

"Why?" I asked, surprising myself with my annoyance.

"It is his club," she said. "Carcine is adored here."
Figures, I thought.

***

It was Aponi's turn to watch the Planet Hope coordinates. She leaned back in her chair, awaiting what was sure to be a short night. Some of the other Outkasts headed to the City, and she volunteered to watch the configurations. The steady sequence of beats was the first to alert her. The beeps were speeding up in rapid succession. Aponi stood over the pit to get a better look. Red meshes of coordinates resembling red bees were aligning in an arrow. Something big was coming in. Aponi tried to send signals to Carcine telepathically. Hopefully, he hadn't arrived at Rhiannon. The club's walls and frequencies blocked telepathy, a

174

safety feature Carcine inserted for reasons the Outkasts didn't understand.

***

The makeshift camp in Sebastian's Cave wasn't fancy, but Dexter was able to engineer a tracking system. His eyelids were heavy, but his eyes stayed glued to the monitor for any change in atmosphere. He saw the same succession of beeps that alerted Aponi. Carcine didn't get the message, but Dexter did. He wiped his eyes and stretched them wider. "She's found them," Dexter cried, as he stared at a monitor.

Lagos and Diva rushed to the screen. "Call the others," Lagos told Diva. There was no need. Sui Lee opened her eyes and flew out of her black tent. This would be one for the history books.

Chapter 34

Don't Leave in Summer

Rhiannon was at the top of the city's tallest building, hovering on the 290th floor. Carcine had a large flying car that could fly "warp speed," he bragged, whatever that was. But he cruised it slowly, attracting the stares of passersby. He flew low; he flew high. Apparently, he wanted everyone to see us. So much for being low-key.

"Adds to the story," Carcine said, who professed that he was recording the entire night. Delta ate it up, sitting on the back and smoking his smelly stick as the bright lights of the city blurred beside us. The rush of this life was engaging, hypnotizing. No wonder Carcine had forgotten about Planet Hope. How do you wage a revolution from this vantage point? I wondered. But I was very conscious that we had a mission, even if everyone else was entranced by the dazzling lights. Carcine pulled the car onto a deck on the top floor. "The line snakes all the way down to the first floor," Carcine said. I looked below and saw the dots of people standing at the building's entrance.

I've never seen so much light in my life. Even the nighttime gleam from Obama City's gleaming towers of my childhood weren't as bright as the light that flooded the deck. A man in a black suit with two triangles at his neck escorted us inside.

We walked through a dimly lit hallway and entered what Carcine called his private paradise. I have seen spectacle before. Moulan's old-world haunts, the faint memories of Shogun City were fascinating, but none had the energy of this large black room, whose frenetic energy pulsated like dark matter. The ceiling was the night sky. Lights peppered the place, but the swirl and the throbbing dancing stirred the place into a spinning whirlwind of euphoria. The music was audible electricity. We were dancing under stardust."

"Have you seen anything like this before?" I whispered to Delta.

"Never," he said. Carcine ushered us to a plush balcony, where we could watch the fun. He handed us goblets and urged us to "drink up." But I wasn't interested in this private scene. I wanted to go to the floor. I shared this with Luba. Her eyes danced.

"Yes, yes," she said. I grabbed Delta's arm and we followed Luba.

This sea of people moved in harmony. Couples slinked like snakes, others popped frenetically. Luba led us to the center of the dance floor. "I will be back," she said. Seconds later, she was atop a podium, slithering to the rhythm.

I danced, too. Delta did as well, and for some time we were lost between beats. Where is the Crystal Cove, I asked myself? I thought of the elaborate structure in Carcine's abode. Did the Neo Astronauts make it, I wondered? Were they creating a mode to go back home? The original technology was created by some of their incarnates. Surely there was a relationship. I danced and danced and the questions persisted. But then an odd thing happened. The rapid-fire questions evolved into equally fast revelations. The vibrating room was a blur, and I was alone in a sea of lights, crystal lights. I was the beat and the notes in between. I thought of the cave, the mysterious words; and suddenly I was transported back into that room, the ancient symbols swirling around me until finally these weird etchings whispered their meaning. "The Crystal Cove is in me," I gasped. That's why Moulan feared me. That's why the Shangos trained me. That's why the Ladies of the Enchanted Forest protected me. Was I the bridge from this world to the next? Was I the healing link to a fractured string? The roar of the words was so euphoric I almost collapsed, but Delta caught me. I passed out.

Chapter 35

A Thousand Smiles Keep Me Lit

I awakened in a white room, clutching my sword, ready to fight.

I do not know where I am. U whispered in my ear. "Get ready," she said. "I cannot shut this off." She vanished. A faceless figure shrouded in white cloth held his gleaming sword as well. He slid effortlessly like a cat, a white cat.

"Who are you?" I shouted.

"I'm who you've been looking for. Who you've been running from," he said, the voice felt like sticky oil on my skin. A fleet of Tigers appeared, running for me. I swung my sword wildly, but they vanished. I was gripped with fear. Sweat poured from my temples, and I gripped my handle harder to minimize the shaking. I was facing the Dirk.

"Did you really think you could outrun me?" he said. I anchored my stance. I was so afraid. Where was everyone?

"Planet Hope must be free," I said, forcing power through the trembles.

"Are you afraid of me?" he said, as tentacles grew from his sides. I closed my eyes, trying not to be rattled by the grotesqueness. "Or are you afraid of yourself?" he asked. I didn't respond. What an odd question.

"Answer me!" it screamed. I aimed my sword for its heart and the Dirk screamed, stepping back and repositioning for his blow. We fought and fought, our skills equally matched. His force was greater, but I was more nimble, ducking, blocking, and running in this endless space of whiteness. He was, it seemed, everywhere and nowhere at the same time, as if I were fighting many men in one. In the whiteness, I somehow cornered him and he vanished. I spun around to face him, and he toppled me to the ground, a sword at my throat. I gasped for breath, the loaded pressure on my neck nearly unbearable. I looked at the black hole in the white cloak, looking for some semblance of a human. Then my mental lightbulb popped. This Dirk was not human. In fact, this Dirk was not real. This space was not real. Was the takeover of our planet waged by the unreal? Was I dreaming? I grabbed my knife, the guardian knife that Luba gave me from my side.

"You are not real," I gasped, the words barely escaping. "You do not exist," I said, wrestled my remaining energy enough, and stabbed this non-thing in the head. It vanished like the Tigers. The world of white collapsed.

I was back on the dance floor, still wiggling to the music. The blurred faces in the blackness took shape. Delta was still in front of me. Luba was still on the podium. I held Delta and whispered in his ear.

"Delta, the Dirk is not real," I said. He was lost in his own groove and could barely hear me.

"What?" he shouted. He didn't hear me and perhaps Delta didn't need to. This was my own private victory.

That's when I saw them. A man in all black on the other end of the crowd standing before a door. He was joined by two women, in all black as well. Stealth and silent, they were not parties to fear. They were family.

"Delta," I whispered. "They're here. The Neo Astronauts are here." I took his hand, and we snaked through the masked crowd toward them; but my father and friends glided behind a bar and disappeared.

Someone whispered in my ear. "We must leave now," the voice said.

I whirled around. "Dad," I said. The glowing eyes, the strong cheekbones, and pug nose were masculine mirror images of my own.

"Follow me," he said. Delta and I followed him. I waved to Luba, who was twisting about on the podium. I caught her eye, and she leaped into the crowd. I looked towards the balcony for Carcine. He was swaying to the music, eyes closed, intoxicated by the rhythm. Shouting his name would do no good in this sound chamber. Carcine, please look this way. I yelled his name, but my voice vanished in this hall of percolating sounds. Delta pushed me along. I followed Kent to a back door and joined the others.

But our escape was blocked by another familiar face, a sea of red fighting machines. Silverado Diego and his fighting Shangos.

"Kent Illmatic," Diego said.

"I thought you didn't involve yourself in matters outside of Shogun City walls," said Kent. "You picked a fine time to show up."

"Typically," said Diego. "However, this is a matter of extreme security breaching. You are harboring two captives. Rayla Illmatic, I believe we had a deal. But since you've found your way to Earth already, give me access to the Crystal Cove."

"We are leaving this planet," Kent asserted.

"That is not my concern," Diego said. "Turn her over to me." A wind swept through the dance floor. Lagos, Diva, and the other Neo Astronauts rode on its wave, swords drawn.

But I was done with formalities. I pulled out my sword and swung for Diego's head; he ducked, used his mental powers to lift me in the air, and tossed me over the dancing crowd to the other side of the room. Kent pulled his sword and grazed Diego's face, and Diego hurled a battle cry. The Neo Astronauts drew swords, the Shangos drew theirs, and the crowd screamed in horror, running out the front door, as the Shangos filed in.

"You will not be the gatekeepers to the Crystal Cove," said Kent.

"And neither will you," Diego charged. Kent levitated into the air, the Neo Astronauts following his lead, did the same. The Shangos, poised for battle, levitated, too.

"We are long overdue," Diego said.

"You are wasting your time," said Kent. "I am not the enemy."

"No, she is," Diego said, pointing his sword at me.

Diego soared towards me, but Delta blocked his blow.

"Get her out of here," Kent yelled to Delta.

Delta tried to pull me away, but I resisted.

"Remember who you are," I said to Delta. With that, our feet two inches from the ground, we were now battle-ready.

The battle ensued. The Shangos and Neo Astronauts circled one another like honeybees, swinging and blocking as we hovered over Rhiannon. We were fighting to get home, fighting for our freedom. And the Shangos, for some bizarre reason, were in our way. We fought for what felt like hours. Each blow I swung towards a Shango, a memory of a friendship resurfaced. What did I do? I wondered. But my wonderment was the backdrop for a fight to the death. At one point Kent and Diego dropped their swords, relying on brawn and sheer muscle power to overcome one another. Diego had my father pinned to the ground, but I circled back and tackled Diego. Diego wrapped his arm around my neck.

"Really, is this necessary?" a voice said. Moulan, shimmering in green, had a caravan of Tigers behind her. Her presence was shocking enough, but to see her with the Tigers proved an idea I had. Moulan was their creator."

Moulan narrowed in, forcing Diego to loosen his grip. His hand was blazing with heat, and he let go.

"Thank you, Rayla, for locating the astronauts. I am delighted to see you, all of you. It's been a spell."

"You've kept us away long enough," Kent said. "We are going home," he added.

"Here you are, the Shangos and the Neo Astronauts at odds, when you both have the same goal: preserving your dear Planet Hope. Never ones to get the big picture, and then I'm left to clean up the mess. A pity.""The Dirk is not real," I shouted.

"Of course the Dirk isn't real," she said. "You, all of you created the Dirk with your naysaying and your backbiting and your petty fights. You created the Dirk, not me. The only way to unite you was to create something for you to fight against. And that man was going to shut down my program. I took his life, but his tyranny lives because of you. None of you would be here without it. The work continues. The only way to get our planet on track to fulfill its true mission was to start anew."

"That's not your decision," I said.

"And whose decision is it?" she asked coyly. "Yours, Rayla Redfeather, pride and death of the Mighty Shangos. The little lady hell bent on taking over Planet Hope?"

"Never," I said.

"Your boyfriend didn't tell you?" she said. "What a shame. The Shangos and their petty elitism. The Neo Astronauts and their blanket idealism. And the people—all pawns for a government that shouldn't be. Yes, I made the President vanish. Yes, I captured the original Dirk. But the mind surveillance was an accident. If the Shangos hadn't been working on a similar program, I wouldn't have had to create one that was and still is better than theirs. Planet Hope is not supposed to impose on personal liberties; but if we do, it will be under my watch. But you, my dear Kent, your being lost in space was an accident ... at first," she chimed. "Your return would have just screwed it up all over again. And you would have imprisoned me, and I will not be controlled," she screamed.

"You cannot hijack space and time," Kent bellowed.

"And you can't take my child away from me," she screamed.

Her child? Who was her child? The eyes upon me from the known and unknown said it all.

"Did you really think she wouldn't find me?" Moulan said. "Did you think by shuffling her from Sui Lee to the Enchanted Forest to Shogun City and back to those rebels would keep us apart? What were you doing, Diego? Training her to be my murderer? When her powers became as great as mine, you tried to topple her? When she challenged your elitist rule and ways, you imprisoned her, and she still escaped to find me. Neo Astronauts, I took your children because you took mine."

This was the great secret that Delta wanted to protect me from? In all these years, I thought of Sui Lee and the sisterhood as my mothers. I thought of Ms. Delight. Never did it cross my mind that I did not know my true mother.

"Rayla is my greatest protégé. She is what you all could be but will never be because of your closed minds," said Moulan. "The Crystal Cove is within her, just like it's within you; but you'll never understand it unless you come through me. She and I will create this new world. She and I will travel the notes of time. And I'm sorry that the rest of you will not be a part of it, especially you, Kent.

"I will not join you," I said. "This is not right."

"Then you will stay in this time worm with the rest of them," she screamed. "None of you will see Planet Hope again. You can thank me later."

"Your vengeance is not just," said a tall woman at my father's side. She removed her black scarf around her mouth. Was this Eartha Mandela? The smile on Delta's face indicated it was. "You will pay."

Moulan's Tigers flooded the floor and we, the Shangos, the Neo Astronauts, Delta, and I took to the air and repositioned ourselves. But I was still dazed by the revelation. Moulan was my mother.

"Dad," I said, flying near him. "Is it true?" I asked.

"Yes," he said. Diego and Delta joined us.

"She blocked the strings," Diego said. "Even if we beat them, we can't get back."

"And we can't unblock the cove with the Outkasts," Eartha said.

"Returning to Planet Hope won't be a problem," I said.

"Can you get us all back," Kent asked.

"Yes, yes. But we have to get to the blue water," I said.

"We'll cover," Dayo said, whizzing by.

"Have you figured out your strategy yet," Moulan said laughing. The Tigers mimicked her jolliness. But we were not alone in our confusion; Black hovercrafts circled the club.

"This is the galactic police," a loud voice echoed. "Come out with your hands up."

"Positions," Diego yelled. The Shangos forged a force field.

"We must tell them who we are," I said. Moulan soared first, clutching her wrists together.

"Do you remember me," she shouted to the dark hovercrafts. Rising to face the largest one in the front window.

"Now," Diego shouted. The Shangos aligned, covering us as we flew like the wind to the blue water. Moulan saw our escape, and she and her Tigers went after us. The Black hovercrafts were behind them. I raced to the water, cutting through the air at full speed. A fleet of air bikes surrounded me. Carcine, Luba, and the Outkasts were at our sides. The others were in full-scale battle with the Tigers. The confused galactic police, I sensed, were trying to figure out our identity. And Moulan was hell-bent on getting to me. I could see her bulldozing through the Shangos' line of defense. The galactic police were shooting their lasers at all of us, but the Neo Astronauts managed to block the lasers with a force field, while slaying the Tigers with their swords. The Shangos were hurling the Tigers from one end of the coast, all using mind power. The site was almost too amazing to behold.

I got to the yellow shore and stood, trying to claim peace in the madness. In the distance, I could see a fit of green flying past everyone.

"Rayla, hurry," Delta said. I tried to envision faces, all of those who were coming with us. I saw the Shangos, Kent, Eartha, Delta, Diego, Dayo, the Neo Astronauts. With explosions popping around me, I tried to see everyone. Luba,

183

I can't forget Luba. And Carcine. But for some reason I couldn't see his face, I couldn't get his face clear in my mind.

"Rayla," I heard Delta shout, as he tried to refocus me. I took his hand. I closed my eyes, but I could feel the lift, the lightness.

"Noooo," I heard Moulan shout. But her voice was many miles away.

"The ark," I heard Luba scream with glee.

But my thoughts were on the peace of the Crystal Cove, that special isle of love and power within me. I could feel the love encircle me, I relished in its bigness, I felt the light expand, and stretching beyond even the farthest reaches of the many multiverses we'd yet to travel. I felt it all, and when I couldn't comprehend anymore, it all went white.

Chapter 36

The Light Life

I awakened in the field of the Yellow Lady. The sun tickled my face, and the dry grass scratched me. Obama City gleamed, the sunrays bouncing like bubbles off the crystal domes and panes that lined the buildings. Wafts of smoke from food cooking floated from a camp nearby. I rubbed my eyes to be sure my vision was clear. People, adults, and children were lined up outside of Moulan's Cottage, some with books in their hand. That's when I felt the narrow finger poking me in my side.

"Thank you," Rita said, as she kneeled beside me. Her soft pink dress shimmering in the sun. "We are free. Everyone has their own book now. "

"And the people are freed from the caves," Sui Lee said, as she helped me to my feet.

Kent, Diego, and Eartha were chatting with Delta's troops. I walked toward them.

"Sleeping beauty is awake," my father said. I hugged him for what was the first time in years."

"What next?" I asked.

"We establish a new government. We repair our relationship with the new planets, with Earth. We keep an open road between our two planets. Connect the Outkasts with their families." The Neo Astronauts were together again,

185

each of them sitting at a table under a large oak tree. All one big happy family.

"What about Carcine?" I asked.

"He has work to do on Earth," he said. I nodded. That is his choice.

"What about Moulan?" I asked.

"She is no more," Diego said. I couldn't resist the tear that fell from my eye. Eartha turned her head. Kent hugged me. I loved Moulan; and despite all her ridiculousness, I discovered my gift through her teachings. She granted me my greatest wish. She helped me find myself. She helped me save Planet Hope.

"We have a lot of catching up to do," my father said, wiping my tears. I nodded. Yes, we did. But I wondered what happened between him and Moulan? I wondered if he would ever tell me. I hugged him again and sauntered off. I was happy for our world, but more distraught than I thought about Moulan. She was the mother I knew and didn't know.

"Rayla," Delta shouted trotting over to join me. "We did it," he said.

"Yes," I said, realizing the weight of our victory for the first time. "Yes, you're right."

"And we found my mother," he said, beaming like a young kid.

"Yes," I said, realizing the irony in our gain and my loss. He wrapped his arms around me and held me. I couldn't believe that I was crying.

"Don't' worry, Rayla. It's for the best. For now anyway," he said. I lifted my head from his chest.

"Delta, I used to think your gift was that of a warrior's mind and spirit. But I think I'm wrong. There's something else," I said. "I can't quite put a finger on it."

"I'm a man of many gifts," he chimed.

I hugged him again. But Moulan's Cottage was beckoning me.

"I'll be right back," I said.

"I'll be right here," he said.

Doug, the freckle-faced boy in Sebastian's Cave, came running out of Moulan's Cottage with his book in hand, running smack dab into me, and wrapped his short arms around my waist.

"I missed you," he said. I kissed him lightly on the forehead. "I told you you would save Planet Hope," he said. "Yes, you did," I responded. "Sound like you have the gift of sight," I said. He smiled and skipped off to the camp.

Inside, I passed the lines of people and sauntered into these familiar haunts. Diva was helping distribute the books in the library. Delta once said that there was more to claiming your future than owning your own book, a reality that struck me as I watched adults and children clutching to their stories as if it defined their lives. Did it, I wondered? Diva looked my way, a half grimace on her face. I guess I never got around to giving her that update. I waved to her and headed for the aisle with Moulan's many portraits. She was a beautiful woman, a genius, but totally overtaken by personal will. I studied the portraits, looking for motherliness in the watercolors and oils. Diva stuck her head out the library and eyed me suspiciously.

"Are you okay?" she asked.

"Yes. Of course," I said.

Each painting was almost comical in its attempt to recreate a mythical state of narcissism. As I came to the end of the hall of paintings, I spotted that the last painting was actually a mirror with ornate gold frame. I saw myself, this new me who had played a role in bridging this world with the next. I profiled, turning my head from side to side. The frame framed my face nicely. Considering that I'd awakened in a dry field, I didn't look so bad. No bruises or scratches. In fact I had a nice glow, a twinkle in my eye. I brushed hair back off my face. All was well, I suppose. Then I felt hotness on my chest, where the pendant of my necklace rested. In the mirror my turquoise stone was a brilliant emerald green. I looked down at my chest. The stone had changed colors. I stepped back from the mirror and walked quickly down the aisle, past Diva and the line of people and out the door.

"Delta, Delta," I shouted. He was chatting with Eartha by a tent, excused himself, and trotted over. I looked at his pendant. It was green, too.

"Our pendants," I said. "They're green."

Delta looked down at his stone.

"Weren't they always green," he said.

"No they were not always green," I said. "You know good and well they were not green."

"You sure about that?" he asked, his eyes twinkling.

"Delta what is going on?" I said.

"You tell me," he said, chuckling. "This life thing is never-ending. You know that better than most," he said. Diva had left her post at the library, came outside, and was staring at us.

I kissed Delta. Part distraction, part desire, I didn't know quite what to say. What we shared was unexplainable.

Luba ran over to us.

"We're having a dance party," she said. "A great big dance party in the heart of Obama City tonight. A masked ball," she sang. "The theme is the Emerald City," she said with a wink and headed off to tell the others. I was glad to see Luba do the winking. I feared that if I ran down the hall of Moulan paintings they'd be doing the same thing. My satchel at my side felt heavier than usual. I peered inside. No, it couldn't be. A hue of green glowed. Beside my book was another. Etched in gold it read "Moulan Shakur." I looked over my shoulder, both Diva and Anna were squinting their eyes at me now. I walked just beyond their line of site. I breathed in the glorious day. I would read Moulan's book. But first, I will live my own.

Biography

Ytasha L. Womack is an author, filmmaker, futurist and dancer. Her works include the critically acclaimed books *Afrofuturism: The World of Black Sci Fi & Fantasy Culture*, *Post Black: How A New Generation is Redefining African American Identity*. She's also the coeditor of the anthology *Beats Rhymes and Life: What We Love & Hate About Hip Hop*. Her films include *The Engagement* and *Love Shorts*. A *graduate of Clark Atlanta University, she resides in Chicago.*

Made in the USA
Las Vegas, NV
27 February 2021